Michael McLean, both hands clasped to his stomach, turned up an agonized face. His skin was a yellowish gray. A rifle and canteen lay near him. He shook as if cold. He stared at Bishop, who, not dismounting, sat silently regarding him.

At last McLean gasped, "I guess I'm pretty sick."

"I guess you are," Bishop agreed.

"My stomach. It's in knots. Burning."

"What've you been eating?"

"Nothing, lately."

"Drinking?"

"I filled my canteen from a spring."

"Alum spring." Bishop swung down off his horse. He unstoppered McLean's canteen, poured its last dregs into his cupped palm, tasted it, spat it out. "Alum water on an empty stomach. You've done yourself up fine!"

McLean attempted to rise. A spasm wrenched him and he fell back, shuddering. "Tasted queer. I was thirsty. Everything's queer in this hell's backyard. Can you do anything for me, or are you going to leave me here to die?"

I

THE BIG MAN paced on the shaded side of the street, his black coat slung over his arm, and turned in at the livery stable to see how his horse was faring. In the stable he found the summer heat less intense, the ammoniac stench a relief from the thin odor of baked earth.

Before going on to the stalls he stepped back to look along the street. He took note that the town marshal, who had pinned a sharp stare on his pair of guns, had not seen fit to come trailing after him. Just as well.

His black coat, cut almost to knee length, normally hid sight of his guns, but the afternoon heat made wearing it a burden. This dead town, emptied of most of its population by the goldstrike at Aguila, boasted the dubious honor of being one of the hottest spots in Arizona. He was only staying overnight to rest his horse. His tiny hotel room was a stifling sweatbox. The town's two saloons were lifeless, their poker tables deserted and dusty. He had ridden a long way here, a tough trail stretched ahead, and he felt irritable. Given the choice, he would have reached Aguila earlier in the year, ahead of the heat, but the delays of circumstances had prevailed over forethought.

His irritation increased when he inspected his horse, a magnificent black that deserved respectful care. The stableman's rubdown dissatisfied him. He raised his voice. "Let me have a brush and rag here!"

The stableman didn't respond right away. He was trying to sell an old skewbald nag to a sandy-haired young man who wanted something better. "Y'see," the stableman explained, "when the folks all lit out for Aguila last spring they took most ev'ry horse fit to carry saddle or pack. This'n here's all I got for sale. You can have him for a hundred."

"A hundred dollars! Does that include a saddle?"

"It don't. Cost you forty more. Saddles is scarce too."

"It's robbery!"

"I dunno where you come from, but here we don't give 'em away."

"You sure don't!" agreed the prospective buyer.

The big man interposed. "Brush and rag," he demanded, and his tone sent the stableman scurrying off to get them.

With chill politeness the sandy-haired young man said, "Let me point out to you that he and I were in a business discussion, which you interrupted." He plainly was not in a good humor, and he introduced himself crisply. "My name is Michael McLean."

"Mine's Bishop."

"Mr. Bishop, your manners could stand improvement!"

Rarely before had Bishop received such a cool dash of dressing-down, never from a stranger who wasn't a gunman crazy to build a score. McLean's appearance made him a little difficult to classify. He wore woodsman-type boots that no cowman would have been found dead in, yet he didn't bear the stamp of a miner. He had an open kind of face and an educated tongue, but his eyes hinted at a ready roughness.

Bishop, for his part, also presented contrasts. His guns and Texas boots bespoke one thing, while his white shirt and long black coat indicated something else, faintly ministerial. His black, flat-crowned hat was saved from Quakerish severity by the slant of its broad brim, like a monk's treasure that had somehow slipped to a rakish tilt. Under it, his gray eyes glimmered, tarnished silver in a dark face strong with forthright assertiveness that would have been iron arrogance but for its suggestion of sardonic humor.

"Mr. McLean," he said, matching the younger man's formality, "if I interrupted the sale of that animal, then I did you a favor. It's not worth buying."

"I'll form my own opinion, thank you!"

Bishop shrugged. "Never try doing a fool a favor," he murmured. The stableman brought him brush and rag, and he went to caring for his horse.

He overheard Michael McLean beat the stableman down to seventy-five dollars for the skewbald. A waste of money. McLean bought a patched saddle for thirty dollars, then inquired about hiring someone as a guide. Bishop smiled faintly at the query. Another gold-fever pilgrim, probably cherishing a secret map that some bogus prospector had sold to him.

"Guide to where?" asked the stableman.

McLean's vague reply exposed a guardful reticence. "A place in the Vulture Mountains."

"Whoo-ee! Across the Harque Hala? That desert this summer's a *desert*, man!" The stableman went on to say that only an old-timer would venture the trek since the onset of scorching sun and sudden sandstorms. All the old-timers hereabouts had departed for the Aguila diggings before summer, along with everybody else able to swing a pick. "It's damn near a ghost town."

"What is?" McLean asked quickly.

"This here town. Ain't nobody left here fit to cross the Harque Hala in this weather."

7

"Guess I do without a guide, then."

"You know about sand drifts? They've buried the trails. A greenhorn can wander in circles out there till he drops. Or goes crazy chasin' a mirage for water."

"I've got a map and a compass."

Bishop stopped grooming his horse. A fake map and a pocket compass, and the pilgrim fancied he was equipped to set out for fortune on his sorry skewbald. By all odds the Harque Hala would win.

Against his better judgment Bishop called casually from the stall, "It happens I'm making for Aguila. My course'll take me close by the Vultures."

"So?"

Stepping out of the stall, Bishop found that McLean's eyes were cold with suspicion. "So I'm offering to let you trail along with me."

"Why?"

His guns, Bishop guessed, and possibly his hard face, didn't quite fit McLean's idea of a Good Samaritan. And they had started off on the wrong foot. Ignoring McLean's question, he said, "But you'll have to get yourself a horse that's a horse. What you've bought there is a—"

"Want to sell me yours?"

"Hell, no!"

"Then why this interest in my welfare?"

Bishop's temper prickled. "I took a notion to help a fool, that's all."

"That's twice you've called me a fool." A hint of the South crept into McLean's speech. "Would you care to tell me how you came by your opinion?" His hands closed.

"You bought a crowbait to ride the desert. You'd rely on a map to get you to wherever you think you're going. I bet it's a hand-drawn map, at that."

"You sound as if you might be fishing for information."

"No, your map doesn't interest me a bit."

"Purely from the goodness of your heart, you'd help me reach my destination, eh?"

"It's not a habit of mine," Bishop said. His offer had stemmed from something distantly related to the range rule of lending a hand where urgently needed.

"I'm damned sure it's not, from your looks!" McLean shot back at him. "If I ever want a favor from you, or anybody your kind, I'll ask for it!"

The troubled stableman laid a hand on his arm. "Hey, watch y'self, young feller, he's—"

"I can see what he is! I've met his kind in all shapes and sizes! Killers!"

McLean's outburst, Bishop thought, sprang from suspicion and ignorance, plus a reckless temper. No doubt he suspected a sinister interest in his precious map. Through ignorance he saw no difference between gunfighters and gunmen.

Charitably Bishop sought for a few words to enlighten him. The words weren't easy to find. In his two hazardous trades, gambling and troubleshooting, proficiency with guns was essential. He considered himself a gunfighter, one of the breed that held to a code. Still, he had veered close to the edge on occasion, more often of late than in former years. He frowned, absently tapping fingertips on his right-hand holster.

Mistaking the gesture, McLean said evenly, "You can see I'm not carrying a gun, but what good would it do you to kill me?"

That was altogether too much. Bishop's face darkened wickedly. His fist whipped out, and he left the livery stable without giving the floored McLean another glance. A man standing outside in the shade didn't have time to step back, and he got brushed aside. Bishop stalked on to the nearest saloon, where the bartender, after one look at his face, set a bottle and glass before him.

"Never fill another man's bucket till you're asked," Bishop growled.

9

The bartender, correctly presuming that the remark was not aimed at the bottle, said, "That's right."

"I should know better."

"Sure."

"Never again."

"Don't bet on it." The bartender had no knowledge of what it was about, but he had seen everything and he recognized the kind of man he spoke to. "Some of us, we got our own way of lookin' at things. What I mean, you feel you gotta do a thing, you do it. You gotta live up to y'self. But there's a lot o' folks don't savvy. Right?"

"Right."

The man Bishop had brushed against came in as Bishop poured his third drink. He lined himself alongside Bishop at the bar, but curtly shook his head to the bartender's query as to what he would have.

"You're Rogue Bishop, ain't you?"

It was a bad approach. Bishop turned his head and regarded him. The man was small and knotty, with a bulldog chin, thin lips, aggressive round eyes. His snappy manner of speaking verged on officiousness. Bishop put him down as some kind of lawman.

He said with slow emphasis, "I'm Mr. Rogate Bishop. Few call me Rogue to my face. Damn few."

"Arno Roone, me. Range detective."

" 'Cash-bounty' Roone," the bartender put in softly.

Bishop nodded. "Heard of him." They spoke over Roone's head, as though he weren't present. "He's the one who packed five wanted men into Tombstone in a bunch. They were dead."

"They're always dead when Roone brings 'em in. Easier to handle and worth just as much. If it's a long way he only brings in their boots. Like I said, some of us got our own way of lookin' at things." The bartender moved off.

Roone hadn't changed expression. "I'm working out of Wickenburg now, for the biggest cattlemen's association in the Territory," he told Bishop. A self-righteous pride tinged his tone. "They got me appointed a special U.S. deputy marshal." He showed a badge briefly and slipped in back into his pocket. "What can you tell me about the McLean feller?"

"He's got a lump on his jaw."

"I saw you hit him. What else?" Roone waited. Receiving no answer, he said, "I got my eye on McLean. He might lead me onto a big haul, biggest I ever went after. You lend me a hand, I'd cut you in."

Bishop drained his glass, still saying nothing, and Roone said, "The ranchers I work for are losing too many horses. A gang of professional horse thieves is stripping 'em. I know who they are and how they operate. I've been working months on it. My bosses have posted bounty on every head, dead or alive, and a bonus if the gang's broken up. It's real money. All right, it's blood money." Roone twitched a shoulder. "Bounty hunting's my trade. I hunt 'em down for their price. I'm good at it. They don't get away from me."

Bishop finally spoke. "What gang is it?"

Roone eyed him carefully. "Gooseneck Starr's bunch. It's not exactly a secret. Starr poses as a horse dealer. He's under general suspicion. I've got facts. I know he makes rendezvous with a horse-thief gang from Mexico. They trade over, and each gang goes back with horses to sell. It's a fast operation—Arizona horses to Mexico, Mexican horses to Arizona."

"Where does McLean come in?"

"I'm not sure. I followed him here from Buckeye. Heard him asking there how to get to the Vultures. His face bothers me. I've seen him before, can't recall where or when. He acts like a greenhorn, but he can take care of himself. He knows I'm watching him. It's making him hot to get out of here."

It went a long way toward explaining Michael McLean's brittle temper and disposition. Bishop shrugged.

"He thinks he's got a map to a goldmine. You've made him suspicious of anybody getting too close to him."

Roone shook his head. "From something he let out today, I think it's a ghost town he's looking for. Wouldn't be any gold left there. Starr makes his rendezvous with the Mexican gang in the Vultures somewhere, most likely near the foot. I got a whisper he uses a ghost town, an old mining camp that played out long ago. I don't know how it connects up to McLean, but it makes him worth tracking."

"If you don't know that country better than he does," Bishop commented, "you're both liable to get lost."

"That's on my mind. I'd be in a fix if he went astray, all trails buried. No water holes left by now, eh?"

"Only some alum springs. I don't recommend drinking alum water."

"Nor me. Twist a man's guts in knots." Roone paused. "You must know a bit about that country. I heard you tell McLean you aimed to go by way of the Vultures."

"Little man, you've got big ears!"

"Part of my trade. Know of any ghost towns there?"

"Never looked," Bishop said. He tapped on the bar and asked the bartender for cigars.

Roone waited until the bartender withdrew. He refused Bishop's indifferent offer of a drink. "I know of a Navajo who I could hire as guide. What I want, though, is somebody fast on the shoot. A man who don't hold back at a few killings where they're needed."

"Go look for him."

"You turning me down? Why?" Roone's face showed genuine surprise. "There's money in it. You like money. You're fast with guns. I know your reputation as a—"

"A man's reputation throws twisted shadows too often," Bishop broke in. "But whatever you may have heard about me, you've never heard that I ever sank to bounty hunting! Your offer is a goddam insult!"

"Well, now, for a man who—"

12

"Get out of my sight!"

Roone turned stiffly and marched out of the barroom, arms rigid, hat straight on his square head.

The bartender observed to Bishop that a badge didn't make a killer any less a killer; it gave him license to kill within the law. "He prowls up in the dark, lays low till daylight, an' bushwhacks 'em cold on the nail. If night never came, he'd be out of his trade. I wouldn't want money that bad. Guess he sees it diff'rent. He acts like it dignified him, dam'f I can see how."

"Makes him feel big."

"It wouldn't me. Nor you."

"We know we're big."

"I guess that's it. I ain't such a big feller, not like you are, but I ain't small inside. That what you mean?"

"Right."

Within minutes Roone returned. He halted inside the swingdoors and stated sourly, "McLean slipped out of town while I was in here, and a sandstorm's coming up!"

"Meaning you won't be able to track him," Bishop said.

"No, but we know which way he's headed. Come on, get your horse!"

"Didn't I make myself clear?"

"As a federal officer"—Roone flashed his badge—"I call on you to render me aid and assistance in the performance of my duties!"

"Request refused," Bishop drawled like a colonel snubbing off a recruit.

"Request, nothing, it's an order and it's backed by government authority! Get a move on!"

Bishop picked his bottle off the bar and let fly in sheer exasperation. Roone jumped back. The bottle smashed on a swingdoor as he ducked out, spraying him in whiskey.

The bartender brought Bishop a fresh bottle, remarking, "Like I said, a helluva lot of folks don't savvy—"

"That one will smell better, anyhow."

Outside, Roone rasped, "I won't forget this!"

"Let's hope you don't," said Bishop.

II

BRILLIANT LIGHT ached the eyeballs while the sun drew its day-long curve across the burnished sky, and the vast silence brought a humming to the ears. Heat waves tortured the forlorn outlines of the sunken flats into a kind of repelling beauty, miasmic and palpitating, through which the dust devils whirled and skittered like crazed phantoms. Shimmering lake-mirages appeared, falsely promising water in the desolation until they faded away.

To the skyline ran the long stretches of sand, splashed here and there by black areas of broken malpais where blue-green saltweed and stunted greasewood clung to a scanty life in the arid soil. The trails were sanded over, no sign left of them. Beyond the skyline on four sides rose the peaks of the Big Horns, the White Tanks, Eagle Eye, and the Vulture Mountains, like heaps of crinkled paper rather than solid rock and earth.

Hungry country, uninhabitable unless some day the rains came. It had a definite air of forbidding trespassers. But Aguila lay to the northwest, and the new gold-strike had put fresh life into that mining town. Aguila meant free-flowing money, all-night saloons, no-limit poker, a fling at quick gains. For that, Bishop had been willing to cross the Harque Hala, a tough trek but the shortest route.

He wore his coat as some protection from the direct scorch of the sun, on the same principle followed by Mexicans in wearing woolen ponchos, removing them only in the shade. Here there was no shade. The black coat lent him more than ever a ministerial aspect, from a distance. He had the brim of his hat pulled down to shade his eyes, though not so much that he couldn't keep track of far-off landmarks. Tall, large-boned, he filled the saddle, the stirrup straps let out to the last notch to fit his long legs.

Two blinding sandstorms had delayed him, costing more water than he could afford, but with care he figured that his two remaining canteens would see him through by a narrow margin. For himself, he could go dry for long spells, but he would not stint his horse any more than he had to; it was bad policy.

At the back of his mind lurked the thought of McLean in those sandstorms. Picking his course toward the Vultures, he half-consciously kept a lookout for him. Becoming aware of what he was doing, he impatiently broke it off. McLean might have got this far, one could never tell. More likely he was lost, wandering many a mile away. It was his concern. He had brought it on himself, that proddy young Southerner, by his bullheaded ignorance.

In the last half of the afternoon Bishop halted to peer at a ragged line of malpais off distantly to his right. His eyes, absently searching again, had fastened on it. Wind-drifted sand had banked up against the malpais, giving the black rocks the appearance of crouched, shrouded figures.

One of the figures moved, crouched lower, then sank out of sight.

Wanting to believe that it was a trick of the heat waves Bishop watched for it to reappear. It didn't. "Hell!" he grunted, and felt only anger. He reined his horse over and rode at a walk to the line of malpais.

Michael McLean, both hands clasped to his stomach, turned up an agonized face. His skin was a yellowish gray. A rifle and canteen lay near him. He shook as if

15

cold. He stared at Bishop, who, not dismounting, sat silently regarding him.

At last McLean gasped, "I guess I'm pretty sick."

"I guess you are," Bishop agreed.

"My stomach. It's in knots. Burning."

"What've you been eating?"

"Nothing, lately." -

"Drinking?"

"I filled my canteen from a spring."

"Alum spring." Bishop swung down off his horse. He unstoppered McLean's canteen, poured its last dregs into his cupped palm, tasted it, spat it out. Its taste was sweetish, faintly astringent. "Alum water on an empty stomach. You've done yourself up fine!"

"Alum? I didn't know." McLean attempted to rise. A spasm wrenched him and he fell back, bent over and shuddering. "Tasted queer. I was thirsty. Everything's queer in this hell's backyard. Can you do anything for me, or are you going to leave me here to die?"

"You asking me for favors?"

"I'm asking you to help me if you can."

"Know any reason why I should?"

"Yes—common humanity!"

Bishop took out a cigar, bit off its end, lighted it. "Common humanity, eh?" He took bleak survey of the sick man. His anger strained and he let it out. "Against all advice a fool goes blundering off into a jackpot, then expects the first man who comes along to throw away his own chances and pull him out of it! For the sake of common humanity I ought to end your suffering with a bullet!"

"Good God, Bishop, are you a man or a devil?" McLean exclaimed. "Perhaps I did play the fool, but it's no reason for killing me. If you won't help, just go your way!"

"All that can help you is fresh water, a lot of it, to flush the alum out of you," Bishop growled. "I've got

16

two full canteens left, barely enough to last my horse and me. It goes against my grain to leave any man to a slow death, but if I give you my water we're both liable to perish."

"I see. Don't you know of any water we could reach?"

"No. Might be a spring or two in the Vultures. Or some water holes. It rains there at times. We could dry up and blow away before we found one. Damn! Damn all greenhorns who'd hit the desert without pack horses, plenty of water and supplies, and a guide-nursemaid! What do I do with you?"

"It's a tough decision, Bishop."

"I don't thank you for it. Want a bullet?"

"No, I don't. I've got out of a few bad fixes, and I'll get out of this one." McLean fought the cramps. Recovering for a moment, he said, "I'll make you a deal. Half share in a fortune, for one canteen of water."

"Half a what?"

"Half a fortune. In silver."

Bishop eyed him with mingled skepticism, cold humor, and pity. Sighing, he unstrapped one of his canteens and tossed it to him. He had known that was what he would do, and had only tried to argue himself out of it.

"You'll be sicker before you get well," he told McLean unfeelingly. "You'll have diarrhea, nausea, cold chills, cramps, and you'll find it hard to swallow. You'll wish I'd shot you. Let it be a lesson to you."

He unsaddled the black and rubbed it down, gave it a little grain, a little water, then sat on a malpais rock, cigar between his teeth, a look of brooding speculation in his eyes. The water was his measured bet against the Harque Hala, and here was McLean gulping it down. It was going to take hours and the other canteen, or most of it, to untie that alum-knotted stomach.

Water. Perhaps in the Vultures. Just perhaps. Tonight, as soon as the sun went down, the trek to the Vultures would have to begin, whether or not McLean was fit to travel. Either that, or tomorrow face a parching day without a drink.

McLean, retching and gasping, crawled off around the malpais, faithfully fulfilling Bishop's list of predicted symptoms.

Bishop finished his cigar. From the inside pocket of his coat he took out a flask and drank sparingly, after which he debated the wisdom of offering it to the patient. He called, "Some whiskey might hurry the cure."

"Don't do me any more favors!" groaned McLean. "I should've chosen the bullet!"

The black's hoofs sluffed through the fine sand, sending up little spurts of dust. Bishop kept pace with his long stride, sinking ankle-deep at each step. A full and luminous moon poured pale light over the Harque Hala and cloaked the peaks of the Vultures ahead in a transparent haze.

Michael McLean straightened up in the saddle and drew the black to a halt. "You ride a spell, Bishop," he said, and dismounted. "I think I can walk now. And I'll have that drink if the offer's still open."

Bishop handed him the flask. "We'll both walk and give the horse a break. He's on slim rations and no water, and that doesn't do his disposition any good."

"A grand horse, best I've seen in some time. Had him long?"

"Since last year."

"Did you buy him here in Arizona?"

"No," Bishop said shortly. "Sort of won him in Texas."

They tramped on in silence, the world empty around them. McLean spoke again presently, but on another subject. "Funny we should both be making for the Vulture Mountains together."

Bishop's eyes glimmered briefly at him over the horse. "Glad you see it that way. My taste in humor runs different."

18

"Coincidence, I mean," McLean corrected himself. "Or perhaps it's not. Back in that livery stable I thought you might be hooked up with a man named Roone who was breathing down my neck. At the malpais I changed my mind."

"Big of you."

"You were right about the skewbald. It gave out on me. Lucky you showed up when you did. You must've been looking for me. I'll bet Roone's looking for me too."

"Most likely."

"Oh, you *do* know him?" Suspicion flattened McLean's tone. "I can't figure out how he knew about the map and the letter." He paused, and asked quickly, "Do you happen to know anything about Clear Day?"

"Sure," Bishop answered solemnly. He had never thought of alum as an intoxicant, but this seemed to be a delayed-action case of it. "We get that kind in this country. One clear day after another. What else d'you want to know?"

"I'm talking about a place called Clear Day, in the Vultures."

"Never heard of it."

"It's where the silver is hidden. The silver that you bought a half-share of for a canteen of water."

"So I did. Hidden silver, eh?" Bishop turned his head and regarded McLean with the half-amused contempt of a hard materialist for a gullible optimist. "Ever try finding the Lost Dutchman Mine, or the Tayopa, or Morgan's buried treasure?"

McLean grinned, his suspicions allayed. "You left out the lost treasure of the Aztecs, sunken Spanish galleons, priates' plunder, and a few more. I took a shot at them too, down in the South and Central Americas."

"You've got the treasure-hunting fever pretty bad."

"I don't want to be poor all my life. This thing ought to set me up. I got onto the track of it when I went home to Kentucky, after my father died. Found it in his papers."

19

"Was he another treasure hunter?"

"Hardly! He was an elder of the church, and raised tobacco for his living. A skimpy living. Yet he knew of a big cache of silver, right there in the Vultures." McLean motioned ahead at the mountains. "I made a deal with you, and I'll stand by it. Half of it's yours."

"*Muchas gracias,*" Bishop murmured drily. "It's lucky for us you pilgrims come in and show us where to look, or we'd die broke! How'd it get there?"

"It's *contrabando* silver. Mexican dollars. Pesos. It was hidden there by some men who jumped a band of smugglers out of Mexico. There was a high tariff on silver, imposed to protect United States mining interests from foreign competition, so smuggling it in was profitable."

"I know. Well, that makes it a bit more believable," Bishop admitted. "It got to be a regular business. Mexican pesos are nearly pure silver, worth more than their face value here in this country. The *contrabandistas* went to using mule trains, slipping up over the border by night, and sold their loads by weight to the right party. The pesos were melted down into bullion and sold on the American market. Profit all along the line. Raiding the mule trains was another business, a lot more profitable!"

McLean nodded. "You believe it now?"

"Not quite. The raiders spent their loot when they got it. They didn't bury it, then go off and forget it. At least, none I knew of."

"These raiders didn't get to spend any of this particular loot. It's hidden on the south side of one of those peaks, near a wide ledge where a mining town used to be. I know which peak, and I know what the town was called. I know, because a black-sheep uncle of mine—my father's younger brother—was one of the raiders!"

Bishop's eyes grew thoughtful. This Kentucky adventurer might not be on a wild-goose chase after all. Nor was he such a fool. Rash, yes, but his rashness in starting out so badly equipped had resulted from his belief that two killers were stalking him. He thoroughly believed in the existence of a hidden hoard of silver; nothing would stop him from hunting for it. It drew him like a moth to a flame.

"Tell me the rest of it."

III

McLean touched his shirt pocket. "I've got it all here, but I know it by heart, every word. Part of a letter written by my uncle to my father. And a map. My uncle went under the name of Sandy Mac after he came West, and seems to have lived a wild life while he lasted. My father said I took after him. He even predicted I'd come to a bad end, like him, if I didn't mend my ways and settle down."

The heredity of family traits was not of absorbing interest to Bishop at the moment. "Get on to the silver," he said.

"I'm getting there. My uncle, Sandy Mac—he was about my age then—joined a gang out here. The gang was organized by a man known as Russian Jack. They captured a mule train loaded with *contrabando* silver. A big haul. Russian Jack had planned it, and organized the gang for that one job. They pulled it off without a hitch. But then they began arguing over shares."

"It does happen," Bishop put in reminiscently. "Go on."

"They split. Sandy Mac objected to Russian Jack claiming half the silver for himself. Some of the gang backed him up, and it came to a fight. When the fight was over, only Sandy Mac and two others were left standing. Russian Jack's horse had bolted with him. The rest were down. It must have been a hot fight to the finish, at

21

close quarters. So Sandy Mac and the other two, Navajo Jones and Billy Red, started north with the mule train. They had a fortune! Every mule in the train carried four rawhide sacks of silver!"

Bishop glanced at McLean, and in the moonlight he saw the shine in his eyes, the feverish hunger for riches. "So?"

"They knew Russian Jack was alive and would come after them," McLean went on. "He was a terror. And there was danger the *contrabandistas* would get help and follow their tracks. The mules were slow. Navajo Jones proposed they hide the loot and come back for it later. He knew a place up Calaveras Peak, where a mining town had gone bad—Bronco City, named after Bronco Rock. Know the place?"

"Heard of it. Never saw it. They hid the loot there?"

"According to Sandy Mac's letter, when they got up to the ghost town Navajo Jones got nervous. The place gave him the shivers. He was part Navajo, and superstitious. He said, 'Let's cache the silver under Clear Day and get out of here.' And I guess that's what they did."

"You guess?" Bishop asked. "What's next in the letter?"

"It tells how they brought the unloaded mules down an old wagon road after working long into the night. They were tired out. Russian Jack fired on them in the dark and killed Navajo Jones and Billy Red. The mules stampeded, and Sandy Mac's horse threw him. He fired from the ground and hit Russian Jack, but in the next second he got a bullet in his chest. The following day some Navajos found Sandy Mac crawling in the desert. They carried him to a hogan. That's where he wrote the letter and made the map. For his gun, a Navajo promised to mail it."

In a minute Bishop said, "That all?"

McLean came out of a reverie. "I was thinking that Sandy Mac must have had more family feeling than my father gave him credit for. He was dying, and he wanted my father to have the silver, but he warned him to watch out for Russian Jack. I guess my father considered the silver as ill-gotten gains. He never did anything about it. Just as well, perhaps. Russian Jack, according to the letter, was a fighting maniac. Those sacks of silver meant everything to him, and he never quit anything he started. He could kill a man with one punch."

"If it's the same Russian Jack I've heard of," Bishop said, "he disappeared years ago. He had an American-born son who lived near Tucson. Got killed in an accident, soon after he married, and his wife died three or four years later."

"From the map, and the description, Calaveras Peak is high and skinny compared to others near it. From a distance it looks as if it rises straight up out of the desert, but when you get closer you can see slopes at the foot, with brush growing on them."

"I know the one you mean. It's over toward the west. If miners built a camp there, they must've had a source of water, probably a spring. Did your uncle say which side the wagon road was on?"

"Yes, the south side."

"Then that's why the camp's been forgotten. There's no reason for anybody to pass by that way. If anything's left of the wagon road, we'll find it. Let me have that letter."

McLean instantly drew away from Bishop's outstretched hand. "Why?"

"I want to read it when it gets light. You may have left something out."

"If I gave it to you—"

"Listen, bonehead!" Bishop barked. "By the deal you made we split the silver between us, if there's any. If it's still there. We're in this together and you better start trusting me. If I had designs on cutting you out, I wouldn't ask you for the letter. Be simpler to shoot you and take it."

"Well, yes, but still—"

"The letter, partner!" Bishop demanded, and McLean slowly drew it from his pocket and handed it over.

The full moon was lowering by the time they angled across the southern slope of Calaveras Peak. Here the sand gave way to upthrusting rock and pockets of soil, dotted with clumps of low cedar bush. On this side the foot of the peak offered no obstacles to climbing, and the two men and the horse, traversing it at a slant, ascended steadily higher.

The horse began straining forward. "Smells water," Bishop said, and they hastened their gait.

The ground fell away, and before them ran a wide wash that carved a winding course up the slope. Grass grew at the bottom of the wash, and the brush was thick. "There's the water," McLean said. "A spring. Or the run-off from a spring up above."

They dropped down into the wash, pushed brush aside, and drank fresh water. McLean filled Bishop's canteens. Bishop, eyes roving, pointed toward the far side of the wash.

"And there's the wagon road. We've about found Bronco City. Big name for a godforsaken mining camp."

The old ruts remained visible. Down on the flats, sand had forever buried the road that once had borne burdens of ore and supplies between Bronco City and Wickenburg, but the higher ground still retained imprints of heavy wheels.

"Let's push on. You want to ride, McLean?"

"It's better I walk. Get my strength back."

They trudged on upward, following the ruts. At a bend in the wash, McLean raised his head and suddenly stopped. Bishop followed the direction of his staring eyes. The slope ended below the jutting rim of a long ledge that evidently formed the floor of what appeared to be an immense cavern, open like a gaping

24

mouth. Above it, a great boulder protruded from the overhanging cliffside, and the moonlight shadows gave it a startling resemblance to a horse—a plunging horse, head slung low, huge neck and back arched in a mad, bucking leap.

"You mentioned Bronco City was named after a rock," Bishop said. "There it is. Bronco Rock. What did you expect, a jackrabbit?"

"I've seen some queer rock formations, but nothing to touch that," McLean returned. "From down here it looks almost alive. I suppose it's the moonlight. No wonder Navajo Jones got the shivers!"

"Been there a long time, maybe a million years. I don't look for him to choose this night to finish his jump."

Bishop led the black on up the wash, which shallowed out wider as it grew more rocky. The ruts faded to traces, but another trail caught his searching attention, a beaten trail that cut in from left of the wash. Stunted cedar threw shadows on it. He paused to decide if it was old or new. He bent, peering down, and blinked once when he made out the deep scar of a mammoth hoof in solid rock.

From a cedar clump came the quiet little snick of a drawn gun-hammer.

Bishop's reaction was instantaneous. He wheeled and ducked low, his right hand slicing under his coat and out again with a long-barreled gun. A shot roared at him. He ended his dive into the cedar bush and lay motionless. In a minute, hearing nothing, he eeled onward, rounding the spot where the shot had come from.

McLean had flattened to the ground with his rifle. He called, "Bishop, are you hit?"

Not answering him, making no sound, Bishop crawled slowly on until he estimated he was behind the unseen shooter. That the shooter stayed silent, unmoving, tokened steady nerves or else a belief that he had made his shot count. Bishop glimpsed the dark huddle of him in the cedar. He didn't fire, though not from charity. A dead man could tell him nothing, and there were things here he wanted to know.

The man sensed that he was being stalked, for he began twisting his head from side to side. He started turning all the way around. Bishop picked up a chip of rock and flipped it purposely short, between his quarry and himself. The crouched figure whirled toward the sound, hesitated a second, then turned his back on it, reading it as a stale trick.

Bishop rose and leaped. His gunbarrel slashed through twigs and struck the man as he whirled again. "No, I'm not hit," he called to McLean. "Come here and look at what we've got." He was brushing off his clothes when McLean found him.

McLean looked down at the sprawled figure. "Dead?"

"Not with that thick skull of his. It's Roone, damn him! Drag him out."

"How did he know I'd come here?"

"You? It was me he shot at!"

"But how did he know?"

"He figured it out you were headed for a ghost town in the Vultures. Maybe Bronco City's the only one there is. He got it in his noggin that you had a tie-in with a couple of gangs he's after for their bounty. Horse-thief gangs."

"So that's why he kept after me! I thought it was Sandy Mac's letter he wanted, though I couldn't imagine how he knew about it."

"Sandy Mac—that's it." The comment came from Roone. He sat up, feeling his head. His frosty eyes, round and unwinking, bored at McLean. "Thought I'd seen you before. Couldn't think where or when. I went after Sandy Mac a long time ago. One of the few I missed. You look like him. Any relation?"

"My uncle."

"Huh. You'll be on the list some day, judgin' from the company you keep! Where's my hat?"

Bishop kicked Roone's hat to him. "You took a close shot at me."

"Didn't know it was you. Thought it was somebody prowlin' up on me. I got enemies, all kinds."

"Don't count me among your friends, if you've got any," Bishop said. "I think you're lying. You're a mean little bastard who'd kill for a grudge or a dollar."

"If I'd known it *was* you," Roone flared, "I would've shot quicker!"

A saturnine smile creased Bishop's lean face. "You could pick up your gun and try again," he suggested gently. "It's right there by you."

Roone ran a glance down to Bishop's empty hands. He shook his head. "I only bet when the chances are right. What're you here for?"

"Water. You been up to Bronco City yet?"

"No. Been scoutin' the lay. The road runs round up over the end of the ledge. But I guess you know. Thought I heard somebody singin' a while ago. Sounded like a woman. Maybe you know about that too."

"No, I've never been here before," Bishop said. "Nor has McLean."

"Am I s'posed to believe that?"

"You can believe any damn thing you want."

McLean, raising his rifle, muttered, "Watch out, Bishop, there's somebody else in the brush!"

Bishop drew a gun. "Got company with you, Roone?"

"Only the Navajo I hired to guide me here," Roone said. "He promised he'd take me to Bronco City, and I had to pay him high for it, but he wouldn't go any closer'n this. Come on out, Vaquiu!"

The brush rustled and a Navajo man came forward, red band around his head, hair clubbed in a knot at the back, deerhide moccasins on his feet, and his blue shirt drawn in with a woven woolen belt. Stocky and muscular, heavy-browed, he didn't look like a coward. Navajos could be sullen, surly, uncommunicative; as racial cousins to the Apaches they rarely were timid. Yet fear glazed his black eyes and yellowed the copper of his skin.

"It ain't you he's scared of," Roone told Bishop. "He's been scared blind since we got here. Navajos don't like this place. They say it's *doyashon*. That means haunted, or bad, far's I make out. Crazy superstitions they get."

The Navajo stepped gingerly around a dim old wagon rut, and gestured vaguely. "*Kleea veitso betay!*" he whispered, and shivered. His lack of silver jewelry marked him as a man without wealth. High pay had tempted him to act as guide to an accursed spot.

" 'Footprints of the Horse God,' " Bishop translated loosely from the whispered words. "I saw one. I'd have to see that stone horse clumping down here, before I'd believe he made it."

"Sure!" Roone snorted. "There's an explanation for everything. The singin' was prob'ly the wind."

"Singing?" McLean asked. He hadn't heard Roone's previous remarks.

"A singin' woman. Pah! There ain't a woman in thirty miles o' here."

"There's no wind either," Bishop commented.

Roone dismissed that fact with a contemptuous shrug. "Don't ask me to b'lieve it was a ghost. That's for Vaquiu. His sand ran out when he heard it. Me, I only b'lieve what I see, and I don't ever expect to see—"

He stopped short in mid-sentence. His round eyes lifted to stare upward. His expression was that of a hardheaded realist witnessing a lie proved true by outrageous reality. Bishop gazed up and cocked a dark eyebrow. McLean drew a sharp breath.

IV

Up on the rim of the wide ledge, beneath the plunging forefeet of Bronco Rock, a light flickered. It brightened. It became blue-green. It threw weird highlights and shadows up the overhanging cliff, making the great stone horse seem to quiver in readiness to jump.

From Vaquiu, the Navajo, issued a mumbling groan of disjointed words: "*Yettso . . . no vahtay . . .* the fire! The fire of the *Dogi-srlaani!*"

Bishop flung him a glance. "The Bearded Man? Who's he?" He looked at Roone. The bounty hunter stood lost in bewilderment. Vaquiu's eyes bulged.

The blue-green fire leaped higher. It illuminated a fantastic figure, a raggedly garbed skeleton of a giant who moved around the fire, tending to it. A mane of white hair hung down his back. A white beard covered most of his face and chest. He bent, poking at the burning logs, building them up to a faster blaze, a piled bonfire.

"Look!" McLean hushedly exclaimed. "Look, he pokes it with his hand right in the flames! My God, he's picked up a log by its burning end and shoved it on top!"

Roone, confronted by the unexplainable, drew his thin lips back in a snarl. "Nobody livin' can do that!"

"Don't you believe your own eyes?" Bishop asked him. "We all saw it." He placed no faith in metaphysical phenomena, any more than did Roone, but he drew a dour pleasure from Roone's bafflement.

"Nobody livin' can do it!" Roone repeated, clinging to obstinate disbelief in the face of visible evidence. The eerie fire-tender picked up another flaming log and arranged it. "It's burning his hand to the bone!"

29

"Then maybe he's not living. Ever hear of zombies?"

"I've heard of all kinds o' crazy things. Never saw one."

"Here's your chance to get a good look."

Vaquiu, moaning low, fled. His moccasins pattered like a stick drawn along a picket fence, and he was gone. Roone took a step after him, stopped, and swore deep in his throat, knowing he could never catch up with the Navajo.

Hoofs struck fast on rock, and from the cedar brush burst a running horse, Vaquiu bent low over its neck. The hoofs presently hit sand and the muffled thudding of them faded away into the desert. The Navajo had quit this *doyashon* place of blue fire, bearded apparition, phantom woman-singer, and the monster track of Bronco Rock. The fact that he had recognized the apparition, naming it as the *Dogi-srlaani,* implied that Bronco City was evilly known to him and his people, as Roone had said it was.

Bishop brought his gaze down from the ledge. "Where's your horse, Roone?"

"In the brush, where Vaquiu had his." Roone's voice sounded strained despite his skepticism.

"I'll leave mine there with it, and we'll prowl on up. We don't want noise."

The *Dogi-srlaani* had raised his wild head at the sound of Vaquiu's running horse. He stood away from the bonfire, peering out over the moon-misted desert below. He threw up a naked arm in a beckoning gesture, then again went to stoking up the fire with his hand. Vaquiu must have looked back, seen that beckoning arm, and given way to sheer panic, for a squeal from his thrashed horse floated back thinly from the brooding silence.

McLean and Roone were waiting for Bishop when he returned from hiding his horse. By their waiting he judged that neither of them felt irresistibly impelled to rush up and make acquaintance with the *Dogi-srlaani.*

As they advanced on up the old wagon road McLean kept his eyes fixed on the hairy scarecrow, until he stumbled on a rock.

"Quiet!" Bishop murmured. "He's got ears, you noticed. He heard Vaquiu riding off."

"Pointed ears, maybe," put in Roone, making his tone heavily jeering, to express his contempt for anything that smacked of the supernatural. "And a forked tail. I reckon to take a shot at him an' see."

Bishop threw him a look. The little bounty hunter meant what he said. He had been rattled by the unearthly sight and actions of the *Dogi-srlaani*, so from spite he would shoot him. "No bounty on ghosts, is there?" Bishop said. "You take that shot, it'll be your last!"

Roone's lips twisted. "He a friend o' yours?"

"I don't know yet. You're not, I'll tell you that."

For a short way the wagon road ran beneath the rim, causing them to lose sight of the fire until a rising curve brought them up onto the ledge where it ended against the face of the cliff. The ledge was wider than it had appeared from below. Its floor sank lower than the rim, and at the far end it split, making a gully between two forks.

Abandoned stamp mills and dumped tailings told the tale of hard-rock miners who had bored and tunneled into the cliff for gold ore, until the veins petered out and word of a goldstrike elsewhere sent them rushing off. Most of the town was clustered along the inside fork overlooking the gully, a location that explained why Bronco City had gone forgotten—it couldn't be seen from the desert, because it was set back below the level of the outer rim.

Caved-in buildings notched the rubble-strewn street like broken snags of teeth. Here and there a sagging falsefront teetered out precariously from roofless walls. Empty corpses of saloons and stores listed at angles of weary finality, only waiting to fall and crumble. From the largest building a big signboard survived, hanging upended on a single hook, proclaiming in carved letters that this was The Morning Glory Bar.

An oppressive odor of dry rot pervaded the ghost town, where once men had worked and lived hard, earning money and squandering it, trying with noise and laughter to combat the forbidding silence of the Harque Hala all about them. Bronco City had sprung into being, lasted its span of time, and died. The great stone horse above it remained unchanged, forever stilled in mid-leap. Seen from the floor of the ledge, with the moon low and the blue-green fire distorting the shadowed contours of it, Bronco Rock looked grotesque, a crude caricature all out of proportion, yet the sense of its gigantic presence could not be shaken off.

McLean, touched by the hushed desolation, spoke in a whisper. "I don't wonder Navajo Jones got spooky here! I'd sooner visit a graveyard in the dead of—"

Bishop gripped his arm, silencing him. He nodded mutely toward a white figure coming out from the street. McLean gulped. Roone froze stock-still, glaring at one more phenomenon that passed his comprehension. Then, inevitably, his hand crept to his holstered gun, his answer to all problems.

The white figure was unmistakably that of a girl, hair flowing down her back. She carried a pail. The blue-green fire and the moonlight gave her a luminous quality that outlined her in almost a halo. She walked lightly with a gliding step, like a lithe young Indian. The fire-light, as she passed it, showed her hair to be fair. It shone through her thin white robe, revealing her as most definitely a female.

"There's your singing woman," Bishop murmured to Roone. "It wasn't the wind."

"A girl," McLean corrected him. "A young girl. Here in this godforsaken hole!"

It seemed as if the girl would come upon the three

watching men, but she turned aside without seeing them. She carried her pail into a small cabin, a ten-by-ten shack that was built plumb up against the face of the cliff. A poor cabin, evidently thrown up by some miner who had spent a minimum of time and effort on his living quarters.

Roone released a breath. "What d'you make o' that?" It was noticeable that he never swore, even under stress. He had a prim streak that sometimes went with men of his kind; men of cold blood, innately vicious, who practiced pale virtues to disprove their viciousness. "Was she human?"

"As human as I am!" McLean declared positively, his eyes retaining the vision of her in the firelight.

"We might call on her and find out," Bishop suggested. "The old man's got his back turned."

"Wouldn't matter if he saw us," Roone said. "I could drop him from here."

McLean planted himself before them, rifle level in his hands. "Wait a minute! We're not here to bring trouble to a girl. I won't stand for it!" His stare was tightly challenging, and Bishop could read what he had on his mind.

He would fight against long odds, this young Kentucky adventurer, to protect a girl. Or the ghost of a girl. He had knocked around in many far places and must have skinned through his share of tough scrapes, while keeping his chivalry intact. He was a mixture of cool practicality, rashness, and romantic idealism. It had not disturbed him to team up with a notorious gunfighter in a hunt for fortune. To him, fortune was admittedly his guiding star, the magnet of his wandering life, the flame to the moth. But the appearance of an unknown girl in this ghost town was raising his morals to the surface.

"I said we might call on her," Bishop reminded him. "I said nothing about giving her trouble. Don't be so damned quick to jump to conclusions. And don't point

33

that rifle in my direction. It's not a good way to get along with me!"

He walked past McLean and paced on soft-footed toward the cabin, noting that the *Dogi-srlaani* stood motionless by his bonfire on the rim, back turned to the town, shaggy white head cocked as if listening for sounds from the desert below.

Nearing the cabin, McLean and Roone following close behind, Bishop turned his head to find Roone sighting his gun, ready to shoot the ragged old giant if he gave any cause for it. He sent the bounty hunter a chill stare of warning. Roone lowered his gun, glowering, intolerant of interference; he was a man who liked to work alone, answerable to nobody, fiercely hating the slightest restriction on his actions. He hated Bishop.

The door of the cabin hung ajar. Bishop rapped his knuckles on it, as an ironic sop to McLean's scrupulous attitude toward women, rather than in formal politeness, for the situation struck him as mildly humorous. To knock on a half-open door, in a ghost town that had probably known no visitors in many a year, was calculated to stir considerable startlement in the breast of the inhabitant.

No reply came from within. The weight of his knuckles swung the door wide open. There were no windows. He stepped inside and looked about him at four walls, a dirt floor, a lean-to roof. No furnishings, no girl, no pail. The cabin was empty, bare as a box, not a stick in it.

"The lady's not home," Bishop said. He took out a cigar and clamped it between his teeth. "We don't get to ask her if she's human. What's your opinion, Roone?"

"I don't believe in ghosts!" Roone edged out of the cabin. "There's always an explanation for—"

"Yeah, so I've heard."

McLean ran fingers through his sandy hair, tousling it like a fright-wig. "It's crazy, all crazy! Hoofprints of a stone horse. Blue fire, and an old man shoving his

34

hand right in it. A girl who . . . She came in here. I saw her!"

"So did we."

"She didn't come out. But she's gone. Even her pail's gone. If I was by myself, I'd think I was off my head. I'd think it was that alum water giving me hallucinations and aberrations of— My God, listen to that!"

They couldn't help listening. Shattering the night's silence, a wild, prolonged howl rang out. It continued while the echoes rolled back, rising in volume, reverberating until Calaveras Peak itself seemed to tremble. It rasped the nerves and tingled the hair-roots. McLean leaped to the door, where he jammed with Roone.

Bishop burst out through them, stepping on Roone, and saw the *Dogi-srlaani* still standing on the rim by the fire, his head thrown back like a howling wolf. The hideous cry broke off. The echoes returned it, then silence fell again.

"That's like the yell Sandy Mac described in his letter!" McLean muttered. "Russian Jack's yell! Said it was like nothing he ever heard. Unearthly, he called it."

"I'll settle for that," said Bishop.

"But it can't be! Russian Jack's dead by now."

"You don't know that he is. It could be him. Your uncle wrote that he never gave up anything, and he looks like he's been here a long time."

Roone leveled his too-ready gun. "Russian Jack? I knew of him years back." The howl had stretched his nerves on edge and put him in a sour rage at the howler for doing it. "He was a big troublemaker. We'll find out if it's him."

Bishop knocked the gun up with a sweep of his arm. "I'll ram that down your throat, you shoot it off around me!" he promised. "I've had about enough of you!"

He nodded to McLean. "Go up and talk to the old man."

"Me?" McLean said. "What for?" The idea didn't much appeal to him.

"If he's Russian Jack, and if you look anything like your uncle, he'll show sign."

"What'll that get us?"

"You and I know what we came here for," Bishop replied patiently. "Maybe he's sitting on it. Just watch out he doesn't clout you with a Siberian samovar."

"What'll I talk to him about?" McLean persisted, liking the idea less.

"Choose your own topic," Bishop told him generously. "Go on, I'm behind you."

They moved forward, McLean unwillingly in the lead as spokesman. A few steps from the fire he stopped, cleared his throat, and attempted a casual greeting.

"Hello, there!"

V

THE *Dogi-srlaani* SPUN around in a crouch. He regarded McLean with fierce intensity, searching his face in the light of the fire. Under the shaggy white mane, sunken black eyes widened in a glare of triumph. The fingers of one hand worked convulsively, opening and closing.

"Sandy Mac!"

His voice came in a hoarse, throaty growl. The hooked beak of a nose flared at the nostrils. Muscles and veins of his long arms stood out bunched by the bursting passion in him. His wild glare brightened.

"I knew you would come back here some day, Sandy Mac! It's been a long wait, but I knew, I knew! It drew you back, didn't it? You couldn't let it go!"

"Look," McLean began, "I'm not—"

"The silver! The silver I schemed for! I planned the

coup, every careful step. I picked my men, trained them, staked and outfitted them for that one big coup. Where did you hide my silver, Sandy Mac?" The growl rose to a shout. "Where? Where?"

He leaped, arms outstretched, one hand a fist, the other a shining metal claw. McLean dodged, but the claw caught in his shirt and slung him down, the ancient outlaw on top, and next he was struggling and grappling to hold the claw off from tearing at his face.

Bishop sprang and grabbed the white mane. He hauled the crazed old man clear and slammed him face-down on the ground. It took all his powerful strength to hold him there with a knee dug into his back.

"Cool off, Russian Jack—cool off, or I'll have to buffalo you!"

Russian Jack stopped heaving, Bishop's voice penetrating through his mad fury. He relaxed and lay quietly stretched.

"Woo, that was close!" McLean got to his feet, breathing hard. "I didn't realize I look that much like Sandy Mac. It wasn't much of a conversation, was it?"

Bishop forced Russian Jack's arms behind him. He looked for something to tie them with, and Roone gave him his bandanna. Roone's eyes were pinched in secret thought; he had heard Russian Jack's words about silver, a big coup.

Bishop, before using the bandanna, gazed at the metal claw: a silver hook in place of the missing right hand. "Here's how he can poke the fire without burning himself," he said. "An explanation for everything, eh, Roone?"

"That hook's silver," Roone observed. A flicker passed over his knotty face. "Solid silver. Never saw one like it. I wouldn't think silver was hard enough. Can't temper it."

"You're wrong." It was Russian Jack who spoke. He twisted his head and looked up at them. Cool mockery had replaced his savageness. "Silver can be tempered by patient hammering, after it is annealed. I did it myself, little man, with a rock."

"Where'd you get the silver?"

"A rawhide sack of it was mislaid in the dark by certain men in a hurry. I melted down enough of it to make this hook. The work was not easy, using only my left hand."

"What happened to your right?" McLean asked.

"A man called Sandy Mac shot it to pieces, and I had to amputate it." Entirely self-possessed now, Russian Jack appended reflectively, "I've often wondered what my bullet did to him." His fluent command of speech was that of a man who could bring an education to his aid when he chose.

"It killed him," said McLean. "He died in three days, in a Navajo hogan."

"Oh?" A wry grimace twisted the bearded lips. "That's a pity. I have long looked forward to meeting him once more. You are kin to him, of course. There is a strong likeness. I have never forgotten his face, but when I saw you I did forget for a moment that he would have changed with age. You caught me by surprise. My mind slipped. It does that sometimes. Forgive my attack on you."

"It was natural."

"Very natural, in the light of my feelings toward Sandy Mac! And very natural for you to come here." The black eyes bored at McLean. "The silver cache! You know where it is, and you came for it!"

"I came to look for it," McLean admitted, "but I'm not sure where it is. I guess you've searched for it."

"Constantly. All I found was that one sack. Fifteen hundred silver pesos. There were over three hundred such sacks on the mule train. Sandy Mac and his friends worked themselves half to death, hiding my silver up here. They were drooping in their saddles when I caught them coming down." The glitter began returning to Russian Jack's eyes. "My silver is here!"

"If you've searched all these years," Bishop commented, "there's not much prospect of anybody else finding it." He hadn't used the bandanna, on second thought, and he tossed it back to Roone. "Isn't it possible they cached it some other place?"

"No, it is here!" Russian Jack swept a hand at Bronco City. "They came down the old road. The sack I found had broken loose and fallen from one of the mules. It lay at the top of the road. My silver can be nowhere but here!" He brought a fanatical stare back to McLean. "What did you learn from Sandy Mac? Tell me!" he commanded.

McLean thought for a moment. "I guess you have a right to ask. Sandy Mac was my uncle. He wrote a letter before he died. About the silver." He paused, shrugged. "All right, they buried it under Clear Day."

"Repeat?"

"They buried the silver under Clear Day. Do you know what or where that is?"

Russian Jack wiped his left hand over his eyes. He pressed it to his bony forehead, trying to stir recollection. "Clear Day," he murmured. "Clear Day . . . No. No, I never have known of any place by that name."

"Well, there we go again. Nobody seems to know of it."

"You are lying to me, young man!"

"No, sir. That's what my uncle wrote."

Roone shoved forward. "I think it's the Rooshun that's lyin'! If he found one sack, he found 'em all!"

"Keep your nose out of this!" Bishop said. "It's none of your business."

"The hell it ain't. I don't get all this talk about silver, but I might've known you an' McLean came here for more than water. The Rooshun's my prisoner!"

"Yours? Feller, you're lucky to be alive. Don't push your luck too far!"

"He's my prisoner," Roone repeated doggedly. "I'm after the Gooseneck Starr bunch. Right here is where they make their rendezvous with the Mexican gang, to swap stolen horses by the hundreds. I'm sure of it. There's horse-sign everywhere. The Rooshun's their lookout!"

Russian Jack rose and stood tall, a primitive dignity clinging to him despite his rags. "Well, well, so we have a yapping law-dog with us!" He paid Roone a patronizing smile. "And what more has your sleuthing talent unraveled?"

"That fire's a signal to 'em!"

"Splendid!" the old Russian complimented him. His manner was confident, pleasant. "Blue fire. Timbers from the old stamp mills, you know. The quicksilver that's impregnated in them burns blue. It can be seen from a long way off."

"You admit you're a lookout for horse thieves?"

"Could I deny it to one so clever as you? Their signal to me is a shot. They send a rider forward who fires once and rides back. My blue fire signals that all is clear. I heard a shot a while ago, and the sound of a departing rider. I thought it was the signal. Sorry if the blue fire startled you."

"It wasn't so much that," said McLean, "as the yell."

"Ah, yes. First the fire, then the yell. They serve a double purpose. They keep any roving Indians away. You saw that hoofmark in the rock? I chiseled it years ago, for the same purpose. Hermits"—Russian Jack's smile grew cadaverous—"don't like to have unexpected visitors dropping in!"

Craft and guile lurked beneath his surface blandness. He was playing a part, more frankly self-condemning than was called for. It seemed to Bishop that he was deliberately talkative, prolonging his occasionally elegant conversation to gain time. Bishop wondered what kind of hole card the old man might be holding, to give him such confident assurance.

Roone evidently also suspected Russian Jack of trickery, for he snapped at him, "Turn round an' put your arms behind your back!" He twisted his bandanna into a rope. "I'll tie that hook an' hand together, an' they stay tied till I turn you in at Wickenburg!"

With a breathed oath of lost patience, Bishop made for him. Roone backed off, too wise to snatch out his gun.

"Lay off me, Bishop!" Roone scuttled backward, agile as a monkey. "D'you take up for a lyin' foreigner against a U.S. law officer?"

"In this case I do!" Bishop stalked him to the single street of Bronco City.

"I'm a U.S. special deputy marshal!"

"You're a damned nuisance!"

Roone made a break to turn and run. Bishop swooped, picked him up bodily by his thick neck and the seat of his pants, and glanced about for a suitable spot to deposit him.

The Morning Glory Bar stood handy. Its rear storeroom, built on the brink of the chasm, had collapsed. The rotted floor tilted downward like a steep chute into space. Bishop raised the squirming Roone higher above his head.

"Slide, roll, or jump?" he queried.

Below the outjutting wreck of the storeroom floor, the side of the chasm lay covered under a thick crusting of broken bottles. The Morning Glory Bar had used the chasm as a convenient dump for its thousands of empties. Without doubt, Bronco City had been a hard-drinking town while it lasted, and the Morning Glory had drawn a big trade.

Roone looked down at the mounds of broken glass. The attraction of the Morning Glory might have come from its having the only girls in town; there were champagne corks in the debris, though not nearly enough to cushion a man's fall. He let out a yelp.

"Bishop! Don't!" He still wouldn't curse. The broken bottles represented to him a depth of human weakness, a vice to be shunned. Feared. It was said that he attended church.

"You going to behave?"

"Yeah! Let me down!"

"Keep your bounty-hunting nose out?"

"Sure! On my oath! Godamight—"

"From you that's blasphemy." Bishop tossed him into the cobwebbed barroom, via a gaping hole in the wall. He walked back to the fire, leaving Roone to crawl out.

Russian Jack offered him no thanks, nor even took his eyes off McLean. Pursuing his delaying tactics, he asked, "May I oblige you by explaining anything else?"

Taking him up on the offer, Bishop said, "You may. For one thing, who's the girl you've got up here?"

Russian Jack's face went blank. "Girl?" He met Bishop's eyes with a masked stare. "There is no girl here. I live alone, the crippled old hermit of Calaveras Peak." A trace of whining senility came into his voice, entirely false; a hypocritical bid for sympathy.

"I exist on the few pesos that are left in the sack. Once in a great while I tramp to the trading post at Cerrogordo Mine. My wants are few. Ah, well." He dismissed the subject. "I warn you to leave this place. Take the law-dog with you. I am not ungrateful for what you did to him, or I would not warn you. If you stay, you will die!"

He turned back to McLean. "Tell me where my silver is hidden. It can do you no good. You would never live to take it."

McLean shook his head. "I've told you all I know."

"You are lying!"

"No, but you are," Bishop put in. "About the girl. You know she's here. So do we."

The ferocity rushed back into Russian Jack's face. "No!" Failing in his attempt to sidetrack that forbidden subject, his recourse was to go berserk. He raised the silver hook to strike.

McLean prodded his rifle at him. "Steady! Cut out the acting. You're lying, all right. We saw her. She wore something white, like a sheet. Long hair, kind of light copper, wavy. About five-foot-four. Slim, but not thin. Er—shapely, I mean."

His powers of observation were excellent, Bishop thought, at least where the girl was concerned. Had a sharp eye for salient points and details.

"Bishop, do you reckon he could be holding her here for ransom? He admits he's running a rendezvous for two gangs of horse thieves. He's been a *contrabando* raider and hell knows what else. He might've kidnapped her somewhere. Or one of the gangs did, and he's keeping her for them."

"We'll know when we find her."

"Old man, talk!" McLean pushed the muzzle of his rifle against Russian Jack's chest. "Where is she?" His own dark speculations regarding the girl's situation and welfare had aroused in him a strong surge of outrage.

A gun boomed somewhere above them, stirring deeptoned echoes like rolling thunder in a well. The bullet chipped rock inches from McLean's feet and screamed off.

"She's given us a pretty fair hint," Bishop said, moving away from outlining himself in the firelight.

Roone came running, hatless, brushing cobwebs from his close-cropped hair. His encounter with The Morning Glory Bar had embittered his prickly disposition to where he craved to kill somebody.

"Up there over Bronco Rock!" he yelled, and fired. "I saw the flash! Use your rifle, McLean!"

43

"Drop that!" Bishop barked at him. "It's the girl."

"I don't care who it is!"

"Didn't shoot at you, did she? Put your gun away!"

"An' let her go on shootin'?"

"Sounded like an old muzzle-loader to me. It'll take a little time to reload. That was only a warning shot, so cut out the gunplay."

In a rage of frustration Roone stamped to Russian Jack. "You old sidewinder! I'll drag you to—"

A call came down, distinct in the clear air. "If you harm Grandy I'll kill you!" A girl's voice.

Grandy. Bishop looked at Russian Jack, trying to picture him as a grandfatherly old gaffer. Grandy. It sounded improbable. Still, he'd had an American-born son, and the son had married. Some of the gaudiest daredevils led private lives of quiet domestication. At some time Russian Jack had courted, married, begot progeny, and had a home-life for a while.

Roone blazed two shots upward. Promptly the muzzle-loader answered him, the flash of it spearing from the black shadow above the stone horse.

"She's quick," McLean commented, angrily relishing Roone's pained grunt. "Quick to reload and let fly, bless her heart!" He removed the muzzle of his rifle from Russian Jack, who, thinking he was about to use it, slapped at it. McLean shook his head. "I won't shoot at her. I couldn't be made to do it."

Blood dripping from a cross furrow in the flesh of his forearm, Roone sprinted off, surprisingly fast on his short legs. He made for the ten-by-ten cabin beneath Bronco Rock, firing up as he ran, like a warrior storming a fort.

"That murdering damned bloodhound!" ground out McLean, and started in pursuit. "I'll stop him!"

"Let's hope he does it right," Bishop said to Russian Jack. "I should've done it before this. My error. But I can't make Roone draw on me."

"Why try? Put a bullet through his head! He'd never know it."

"I'd know it. Come on, you and I'll stick close together." They walked side by side toward the cabin. "Don't try ramming your hook in my neck, will you?"

"No. I'll need you to hold Roone in line, if the young man doesn't kill him."

"That's right."

VI

THEY ENTERED the little cabin to find McLean and Roone facing each other in the near darkness like two bristling dogs. McLean's face portrayed his wrathy indignation at a man who would go to the barbarous lengths of taking shots at a girl. He held his rifle in both hands, finger on the trigger. But Roone was letting his gun hang loose, averse to a shoot-out at close quarters, and McLean would not fire.

Bishop shoved through between them, seeing it was a stand-off, whereupon Roone holstered his gun and went to examining the planks of the back wall. Bishop pulled him away and took the task on himself, aware of Russian Jack's attention. He lit a match.

The broad planks were heavier than those used in building the rest of the cabin. They could have served as cribbing to line the shaft of a mine, and he thought that they likely had done so at one time. He banged his hand along the wall to test its seeming solidness.

Russian Jack said in bitter resignation, "The two middle planks. They're wedged together."

"I knew it!" Roone started forward. "Sure, that's how the brat got—"

"Shut up!" McLean held his rifle as a bar, blocking

45

him. "A woman-fighter sickens me! Shut up before I bust your teeth in!"

"Look what she done to my arm!"

"To hell with your damned arm!"

Bishop hit the two middle planks of the back wall. They gave way, opening like double doors, hung by leather hinges on the hidden side. Beyond gaped the black hole of a mine tunnel. Bishop struck another match. Cribbing had been installed to shore up walls and roof of the tunnel where the rock was loose. The cabin had been built to cover the mouth, probably to guard the claim from gold thieves. Bishop guessed that Russian Jack had added on the back wall to form a hideaway in case of need, and carefully removed all traces of the mine's existence.

"You lead the way," he told him.

"Wait!" McLean objected. "She called him Grandy. If she's his granddaughter—"

"She is," Russian Jack said. "My son was her father. I brought her here from Tucson after she became an orphan."

"It's not much of a place to raise a girl in!"

"Better than the charity of strangers. They put her in a foster home. I stole her. I have been her guardian and teacher."

"We don't have any right to force our company on her, Bishop."

"She didn't have no right to rip my arm!" blared Roone. "She fired on a federal law officer!"

Russian Jack slid a gaze over them. Again Bishop caught an astute gleam in the sunken black eyes. The friction among them suited the old man, and he had heightened it by subtly enlisting McLean's sympathy. The girl's hiding place was exposed, but he would turn it to advantage if he possibly could. He was half-mad, obsessed by the quest for the missing silver, yet able to make shrewd use of expedients. Without a word he ducked his head and stepped into the mine tunnel. Bishop followed, Roone behind, McLean in the rear.

The tunnel became an incline of many bends, a drift that had followed the vein into Calaveras Peak. Russian Jack hurried onward with the ease of long familiarity, the three men groping their way after him in the darkness, falling behind and bumping into one another. If the drift had split, Bishop would have suspected the old man of losing them, but there were no cross shafts.

"Where's the old devil gone to, Bishop?" Roone called. "Did you let him get away from you?"

Bishop didn't trouble to reply. His foot met an obstruction and he sprawled. Muttering pungent words to himself, he struck a match. He was at the foot of a crooked stope, so steep that stairs were cut roughly into its rock floor. There was ventilation, for the air was not stale. He dropped the match and started up the stope.

He heard Roone blunder into the bottom steps and then McLean fall over him, a minor gratification. They briefly discussed the mishap, McLean calling Roone a goddam fumblefoot, Roone grunting something less profane. Sooner or later those two would cross the line; they were building up to it, and McLean stood to lose. His scruples were a handicap against Roone's uninhibited methods of manslaughter. Well, one had to pay for luxuries . . .

Climbing up the uneven steps of the stope, Bishop rounded a bend and sighted a pale reflection of light above him. He climbed on, thinking of the waiting old man and the girl. Russian Jack surely had a card up his sleeve. His erratic brain might or might not prove capable of playing it to its full value.

One more bend, the last, and the pale reflection of light changed into a limited view of stars. At the head of the stope Bishop came out into a shallow cave the shape of an upended clamshell. Here the vein had ended, and with it the workings, the life of the claim. The diggers had drilled test-holes all over the cave, found nothing more, and abandoned the worked-out mine. On the floor of the cave there were evidences of temporary occupancy: a cot, a pail of water and a tin dipper, and a small handmade table.

As his head rose above the level of the floor Bishop looked into the muzzle of a rifle, held by the girl in white, Russian Jack beside her. The white robe and flowing hair gave the girl an unreal and intangible aspect, as if she might float off and vanish into nothingness at a threatening gesture. The rifle, a muzzle-loader, looked incongruous in her hands. She obviously knew how to use it, though.

To offtrack her from using it on him at first impulse, Bishop inquired, "Where d'you get the powder and ball for that piece of hardware?"

His casual tone elicited an automatic response from her. "We have a keg of gunpowder and some lead down in—" She stopped. "Put up your hands!"

Bishop showed his hands, stepping on up into the cave with slow care, distrusting the combination of a frightened girl and a loaded firearm. From the cave's mouth the night-grayed expanse of desert could be seen far below; it merged without visible horizon distantly into the starry sky. The moon had gone down behind the Vultures. A straggling patch of cedar at the mouth screened the ledge from sight and helped hide the cave itself.

"Couldn't you get a better boudoir than this musty roost? It's got a view, that's all I can say for it."

The question and criticism reacted on Russian Jack as a slur aimed at his guardianship of the girl. "We live in part of a building near the Morning Glory," he stated in defense. "We are not animals! It is not a lair."

"This is."

"We use this only in emergency."

Bishop mulled it over, picturing the two of them living in one of the broken-down buildings of the ghost town, prepared any minute to dart into hiding. A primitive animal-like existence, despite the old outlaw's defense of his guardianship. Hideously lonely for the girl.

"What was the emergency tonight?" he asked.

"You and your friends!" said Russian Jack.

"But she came up here before you knew about us. She brought up that pail of water."

"We heard a shot, and somebody riding off. I told you."

"So you did." But the explanation left Bishop vaguely unsatisfied.

Roone emerged from the stope, McLean close on his heels. Thrusting past Bishop, he glared at the girl. "You ripped my arm! Give me that gun, you hellcat, or I'll—"

McLean took a stride, spun him around by his shoulder, and hit him. The punch drove Roone floundering across the cave, where he cracked his head on the sloping roof. He dropped to his knees, mumbling, holding his head and jaw. McLean bobbed a bow to the girl, who lowered the rifle and gazed at him in wonder.

"I apologize for, er, that man. Believe me, we don't mean you any harm."

"Just a neighborly visit," Bishop murmured, reaching for the rifle and capturing it before the girl realized his purpose. "We've moved into town." He placed the rifle on the cot, after easing down the cocked hammer. "Want to get acquainted."

McLean sent him a hard look. He met it blandly, aware that the girl was young and pretty, and of her effect on the Kentuckian. More than pretty. Certainly eye-catching, with her light copper hair, dark eyes, and fine features. And her white robe, fashioned loosely from a piece of cotton goods. She was ignorant of women's dresses and styles, but managed to achieve a

49

natural grace, possibly because of it. Held her head high like a fawn scenting the air. To Michael McLean, romantic treasure hunter, no doubt she appeared as heaven's prize angel on a pearly pedestal, no mortal flaws.

Well, sparkling illusions were fine, in their place and at certain times of life, if a man liked lofty ideals. For his part, Bishop leaned more to a straight flush deviously acquired from the jobbed deck of hawk-eyed sharpsters, a full money-belt, and a good horse. The rest of life's pleasures were all very well, and he enjoyed them, but they were not to be confused with fundamentals.

McLean and the girl kept gazing at each other like two souls alone on a cloud. The girl became noticeably less of a wild thing tensed to run or do desperate battle. McLean lost much of his raffish aspect.

Bishop nudged Russian Jack. "Her name?"

"Tandra. If that law-dog dares to touch her—"

"He won't!" snapped McLean. His stare whipped at Roone, then at Bishop. "Nobody's going to touch her!"

"That's settled, then," Bishop said. McLean was taking in considerable territory, but he let it go for now. He said to Russian Jack, "You went to a lot of trouble fixing up this hideout for her. Was it because you don't trust the Gooseneck Starr bunch?"

"I trust no man, Starr and the others least of all! They don't know of Tandra's existence. They think of me as a crazy old hermit who is useful to them. I play the part. A desert rat who has forgotten his name. They call me Whiskers. If they knew of Tandra—"

"Then you must've had this ready before they came."

"Yes. A precaution. Tandra used it the first time they came. I greeted them at the top of the road. They looked the place over. It suited them. They let me stay on as their lookout, and gave me some flour and bacon. We arranged about the signals. They have come here several times since then."

Roone got up off his knees. "When's the next time?" he demanded.

Russian Jack ignored him. "Now that you have seen this private place and met my granddaughter, won't you leave in peace?" he asked McLean, picking him as the one most likely to comply with an appeal to chivalry.

"We should, Bishop. Let's go now." McLean inclined his head to Tandra. "It's, er—I'm very glad to have met you. Hope we didn't bother you. Roone!" His rifle covered the bounty hunter. "We're leaving!"

Roone took his hand off his low-cut holster. "Young feller," he rasped, "you're headin' for a big fall! I don't take orders from any—"

"We're leaving, aren't we, Bishop?"

Bishop looked at Russian Jack. "I don't see any reason why not," he said, and perceived relief flood into the gaunt face. Relief, and a measure of sly triumph.

The four men moved toward the stope, leaving the girl. The sound of a shot halted them. The shot came from out of the desert below. Russian Jack drew a quick breath, and Roone pulled his gun on him.

"There's the reason why not, Bishop! The Starr bunch! He's been expectin' 'em tonight. He strung us along, stallin' for time, so's they'd nail us!" Roone turned on McLean. "How about your highfalutin' manners now? He was settin' us up for the kill!"

McLean stepped to the mouth of the cave. "It's getting light. There's movement out there." He raised a hand for silence. "Listen, you can hear them coming!"

"How many ride with Starr?" Bishop asked Russian Jack.

"Twenty or more. They saw my fire, so they came on. They will wait below for my call." The old man's face twitched. "It's too late for you to get away. They'd see you on the road. I warned you to leave, or you would die! But you stayed." His speech had grown

51

jerky, uneven. Control was slipping from him. "You found this hiding place. You found Tandra."

McLean shook his head in bewilderment. "And for that you'd try to get us killed?"

"To stop your tongues from wagging! Especially Roone's!"

"I got a mind to shoot you!" Roone growled.

Bishop shunted him off. "They'd hear it." His thoughts raced ahead, probing the potentialities of the near future. "Go on down and call 'em in."

"Bishop, are you crazy like him? Starr's bunch is tough!"

"If he doesn't call 'em in, what then? The fire's burning, so they know he's still around. They'd prowl up to see what's wrong. They'd search for him, and that we don't want. Anybody making a good search would find those two loose planks sooner or later. Use your head!"

"But if he tells 'em . . ." Roone stopped. "No, he wouldn't, would he?" His round eyes rested on Tandra. "We hold her as hostage. If *he* wags his tongue—"

"He understands," Bishop said. "We stay here with her. He calls 'em in. We stay here till they're gone. Sorry to impose, young lady. We'll try not to discommode you. Come to think of it, having our company should be a comfort to you."

He glanced at Russian Jack. "Better than staying up here by herself. She couldn't have slept much, wondering if some joker might accidentally find those loose planks and come exploring."

Russian Jack nodded. "That has been a hard worry to me each time they came."

He worked his strained lips, fighting for self-control. The dementia of a mind fixed for far too long upon an obsession, the silver, lurked close to the surface, breaking through in moments of shock or tense excitement. He evidently recognized his flaw, for before descending into the stope he took deep breaths and forced his face into an expression of calmness. Minutes later they heard his hair-raising howl.

Chewing on the end of an unlighted cigar, Bishop idly wondered if the howl was some kind of Russian battlecry, possibly Cossack. He hoped the Starr bunch wouldn't stay long. Getting cooped up in this roost presented problems. A pail of water, only enough food for the girl, and no smoking. He heard McLean and Tandra talking together, low-voiced. Those two were not worrying. He listened to them, while remembering times when he too had trod the stars.

"I'm the only kin Grandy has in this country," Tandra was saying. She had a rather deep voice for a girl, and used it with changing inflections. "He's very kind to me."

"Yes, but how do you live?" McLean's tone conveyed his conviction that nobody but a monster could possibly help being kind to her.

"We raise vegetables up near the spring, and I hunt. Grandy can't use the rifle very well, because of his lost hand. He spends all his time searching. We'll be rich some day, he promises, and take our rightful places in Russia. But I don't want to."

"You don't want to be rich?"

"I mean I don't want to go to Russia. I was born in this country. I'm an American. My mother was American, and so were all her people. I don't remember my father. Grandy—"

"Is it real silver he's searching for, or did he dream it up?" broke in Roone. He also had been listening to the conversation. The hungry glint was back in his hard little eyes. "Why ain't he found it by now, if it's here?"

Tandra flinched slightly at the harsh demand. McLean swung an angry stare at Roone. "Tend to your own affairs, blood-money man!" he flung at him. "Shove off!" In the next breath he was murmuring gentle reassurance to the girl, who, even if she didn't need it, was receptive to it.

53

Bishop hid a grin. McLean wasn't a bad mixture of a man. Tough enough for any kind of company, but could call up manners to fit a tea party. He could take care of himself. Sandy Mac had probably been that kind of man, but along the trail to fortune he had gone bad. It happened. It could happen to McLean before he realized it.

A hammering of many hoofs rolled up from below. Bishop moved to the mouth of the cave and stretched flat, screened by the fringe of cedar. In the gray light of predawn he could see driven horses swarming up the old wagon road. Their backs glistened. They had been driven hard a long way. Riders appeared.

"They sure lifted a haul o' horses this trip!" Roone muttered beside Bishop. Blows and insults couldn't deter him from business. "How many d'you make it?"

"Around three hundred head. And plenty of riders to handle 'em."

"More'n twenty, all right. Starr's got his whole bunch with him."

The steady roar of hoofs presently changed to noises of horses milling around on strange ground, snuffling and stamping in nervous uneasiness.

"They won't hold 'em there long," Roone commented. "They got water, but not much grazin'. The Mexican gang oughta show up soon with their horses too. It's got to be a fast trade-over."

The riders began drifting into the town's dead street, a stream of them. They spoke little. Hard wariness marked the way they stared about them. They left the street and gathered loosely below Bronco Rock, stretching their backs, hitching up the gunbelts sagging from their sweaty waists, a hardworking crew of horse thieves snatching a spell of ease.

Another knot of riders came in at a canter. Russian Jack walked from his signal fire to meet them, slowly and without any greeting. At their head rode a man

whose bushy yellow hair flared out, his hat hanging back
by its chin cord from his long neck.

"That man," Tandra whispered, "is Starr."

"And well I know it!" said Roone. "Gooseneck Starr
with the goods, an' me stuck up here!"

Starr drew up in a jump alongside Russian Jack. His
arm shot out. The old man's head was jerked savagely
against the saddle by its white hair, and Tandra hissed
as though she felt the pain.

"You old buzzard!" Starr roared. "Who're you hiding?"

VII

RUSSIAN JACK choked out some kind of reply, struggling
to free his head. Starr wrenched him back and forth.

"You're a liar! We found two saddled horses down
there in the brush! Hey, bring 'em here!"

Bishop bit through his cigar. He spat, took a fresh
bite, and cocked an eye at Roone, who met it with a
stiff grimace. In this moment the merciless little bounty
hunter showed the nerve that had served him as a noted
stalker of wanted men.

"A horse can give a lot o' trouble sometimes! I gen'rally
Injun afoot the last stretch."

A rider led the two saddle horses forward. Starr
stuck a thumb at them, releasing his grip on Russian
Jack's hair. "Take a look! The sorrel whickered, or we'd
have missed 'em. Whose are they? If you've got spies
up here I'll roast you over your fire!"

"I am alone," Russian Jack lied calmly. "There are no
spies here. I've never laid eyes on these horses before,
and I know nothing about them. Perhaps they strayed in
off the desert."

"That black ain't the kind o' horse any man mislays!"

55

"Post a watch, then. Its owner may come looking for it."

The riders grouped below Bronco Rock fell to exchanging comments. Their voices floated up to the cave. Some of them were disposed to believe the hermit, arguing that he wouldn't dare cross them, that for him to shelter spies wasn't reasonable. He was just an addleheaded old gaffer, glad of the few supplies they brought him.

Starr would have none of that. "Make a search!" he ordered. "Search all the buildings. Look through all the old mine workings."

"Hell, Gooseneck, we're that tired—"

"Search! An' keep an eye on Whiskers!"

The riders dismounted and scattered out on foot, a few staying to off-saddle the horses and take them to water. Bootheels clacked in the rotting buildings of Bronco City. A floor collapsed, the crash of it mingling with the curses of stumbling men, and somebody laughed. Starr gave a command to Russian Jack, who went obediently back to building up his fire.

"There's a good chance they won't find those loose planks," McLean murmured. "They're not looking for something like that, not a regular hideout."

Roone fingered his gunbelt, heavily studded with spare shells. "If they do, we could hold 'em off. Only one at a time can come up the stope."

"I knew of a man who went seventeen days without food or water," Bishop said, "before he died."

Roone blinked. "Mighty comfortin'!" He wiped a hand over his mouth and crawled back to the pail.

"Go easy on that water. It might have to last us a long time. And hands off the grub! It's the girl's."

"She'll have to share—"

"We won't be here that long," McLean put in, "unless they find the planks. Starr wants the fire kept up, so he must be expecting the Mexican outfit any time now.

You said they make a fast trade-over of the horses. I guess they'll rest a spell, maybe have a few drinks, then go."

"With our horses!" Bishop said bleakly. "Leaving us afoot!" It was that, more than anything, that darkened his mood.

McLean brought up a grin. "I'll be no worse off. I was on foot when you picked me up."

"You were on your face!" Bishop grunted. McLean's cheerful optimism grated on him. Its source was all too obvious. He glanced at Tandra and felt something like a pang of envy, even of regret. There had been a time when he would have cut McLean out of the running for a girl like that.

But that was before poker and cash and a good horse gained top place in his standard of values. Before his two trades of gambling and troubleshooting had ruled out any likelihood of his ever settling down to tamer living.

He turned his thoughts to his horse. It would be sold down in Mexico to some well-heeled hidalgo who'd keep it groomed to a hair and probably parade it around the plaza, all gussied up. A waste of a fine big horse that was built for endurance and stamina. The fact that the black had come originally from Mexico, and would be going home, had no bearing on the matter—nor that he had acquired it in a Texas transaction that skimmed the surface of larceny.

Roone came back from the water pail. "I bet it gets hot up here in the day."

"Yes, it does," Tandra said. "I've sometimes crept down into the mine shaft where it's cooler, while those men were here."

"Hum! That pail's only half full."

"I only bring up enough food and water to last me until—"

"Quite talkin' about food an' water!" Roone snapped, and nursed his bullet-torn forearm.

He wasn't forgiving the girl for inflicting that painful flesh wound, nor Bishop and McLean for their man-handling methods of blocking his violent tendencies. Bishop caught a look in the brittle eyes that set his fingers to tapping on a holster. A necessary killing might be called for before this thing went much further.

The morning sun warmed the night-cooled air. It would be hot by noon. Another sizzling day.

Bishop stretched his long arms and legs, knuckled his eyes, scratched his unshaven jaw. He looked across the cave at Tandra. She slept sitting beside McLean, her head resting on his shoulder. Her face was peaceful. She looked very young, flushed in sleep, faint blue shadows under her closed eyes. McLean, awake, sat perfectly still so as not to disturb her, willingly stoical to bear his cramped muscles.

The protective urge, Bishop thought, could be carried too far. He moved to the mouth of the cave and peered down through the cedar fringe. Starr's men had given up the search and were having breakfast. Bread and dried meat, hot coffee.

"I'm gettin' hungry," Roone grumbled, joining him.

"Chew on your spleen!"

Food at this early hour never interested Bishop. The coffee did. Black, laced liberally with whiskey. His morning bracer. Any morning he had to forego it, that day was off to a bad start.

Roone sourly surveyed the breakfasting men. "It's high time the gang from Mexico got here. They're late. That's Mexicans for you. *Mañana.* I hate 'em!"

Bishop put a biting question to him. "Who don't you hate?"

"He was born with vinegar in his veins," McLean said, and Roone stared at him venomously.

Tandra stirred, waking up. Discovering where her head lay cushioned, she asked McLean with some confusion if it hadn't inconvenienced him. McLean firmly averred that he couldn't have been more comfortable. At that point Bishop closed his ears to them.

"I think they're comin'," Roone said. "Yeah, it's them. They swung round from the west, not the south. Leave it to Mexicans to go anti-godlin'."

"Probably missed their course last night in the dark."

Around the foot of the Vultures moved a bobbing mass of horses, dust billowing behind. There weren't many riders in the outfit, Bishop observed, but beyond doubt they were well mounted and heavily armed. The sun brought flashes from bandoleers brassy with cartridges.

"Them big sombreros sure look foolish to me. A triflin' lot, Mexicans. All strut an' swagger."

"Ever live in Mexico?"

"No."

"I have. Don't let their hats fool you. Keep your head low and don't move. They've got sharp eyes."

The dust boiled to the foot of Calaveras Peak and there hung back, the outfit ascending the slope, and once more the old wagon road thundered to the beat of many hoofs. Starr and his men had risen and they stood waiting. Russian Jack, leaving the signal fire to burn out, walked off toward the street. The band of horses could be heard milling below the western end of the ledge.

"If we'd come up that end, 'stead of followin' the road all the way up we'd have spotted their holdin' grounds." Roone's tone blamed Bishop and McLean.

"Would that have done us any good?" McLean asked him.

"Me it would've. I'd have stopped right there an' took cover, waitin' for 'em. I wouldn't be in this hole!"

The Mexican outfit bulged up and entered the street in a group, swaggering grandly in high Latin mood, voices quick and boisterous. Bishop had met their kind. They

59

lived for loot. By their temperament they could maintain a brooding silence for hours, days. A successful coup uplifted their spirits to the skies. They were more at home in the saddle than on foot, and scant sleep kept their nerves wire-taut. Not one of them was fat. *Hombres del campo*.

Their leader rode a palomino, a choice animal of clean lines, fitted with a silver-mounted saddle and tasseled bridle. In spite of the thick dust on him, he presented a somewhat dashing figure, ornamented in the style scorned by Roone. Beneath his short jacket he wore a pleated silk shirt, once white, and his tight *charro* pants were brocaded down the seams. His pair of lean Spanish pistols flaunted white bone handles. His Sonora sombrero, also brocaded, shaded the slightly blunted features of a smooth face. He had dark, lively eyes, expressive lips, and a thin line of black mustache like the stroke of a pencil. The wear and tear of hard riding and hidden camps had taken toll of his resplendent attire, but not dimmed his innate elegance.

"Damn!" Bishop breathed. His narrowed eyes stabbed down at the *renegado jefe*. "Damn the luck! Of all the horse thieves in Sonora, it had to be him!"

"You know that fancy-Dan?" queried Roone.

Bishop turned a dour glance to him. "I do! And he knows me! You ever hear of Don Ricardo de Risa? On this side of the line he's sometimes known as The Laughing One, alias a string of other names."

"I've seen the dodger bills on him."

"You're seeing him now in person!"

Roone's eyes shifted. His knotty face didn't crack its iron-hard mask. "All that bounty money down there, if I could collect it!"

"Better men than you have tried to nail Don Ricardo. On both sides of the line. He's been hunted by Texas Rangers, Arizona Rangers, posses, Mexican Rurales, and a crack Cordada company."

"What's your worry?" McLean asked. "No reason for him to know you're here."

"He'll know," Bishop said, "soon's he sees my horse."

"I thought you told me you got it in Texas."

"I did. From him! He gets around. So do I."

"Oh, Lord!" McLean scratched his sandy thatch. "You mean you took it off him?"

"Well, there wasn't any bill of sale!"

The black horse stood tethered with Roone's sorrel, among those of Starr's men. It wasn't possible for Don Ricardo to miss seeing it. Don Ricardo de Risa, one-time rebel general, *muy grande caballero*, all-time bandit and horse thief, had too quick an eye for horses. He could spot the black as swiftly as he could spot Bishop, a mile off.

"*Hola*, my friend! *Buenas dias*." Don Ricardo pulled in his palomino. He flung up an arm in an extravagant salute that was as mocking as his speech. "How good it is to see again your honest face, your handsome form, your—"

"Cut out that cackle, Risa, I don't like it!" Starr stuck his arms akimbo, fists on hips. He had an ungainly body, bulbous in the middle, and his long, thin neck, with its prominent Adam's apple, made him grotesque. His face bannered a brutish rapacity. Any compliment on his looks was sheer sarcasm.

Don Ricardo made a mouth. "*Ay, ay!* The common amenities go wasted. Business, strictly business, yes? Very well. I am late because we missed our way. All trails are buried. We—"

He broke off, his restless gaze caught by the big black horse. "*Mi caballo magnífico!* Where did you get that horse?" He added a curt snap of command, his eyes suddenly dangerous, flicking his fingers at Starr. "Tell me, man, tell me!"

Starr's bushy head went back, intolerant and challeng-

61

ing. "Don't take that tone to me, hombre! I ain't one o' your stinkin' *paisanos!*" Those of his men who had squatted at the cookfires rose and stood with the others. They were as far apart from Don Ricardo's type as men could be, and antipathy lay close to the surface.

"*Qué?*"

"You got what I said!"

"I overlook it."

Watching and listening, Bishop observed without surprise the don's prompt change of manner. For all his nervy insolence, Don Ricardo knew when to use discretion. He and his riders were outnumbered three to one. He had been known to take on longer odds, but that was when necessity pressed, or the end was worth while.

"It would be stupid of us to fall out, Starr, doing such a good business together. You take me too seriously. And I am too careless with words."

"You're goddam free with your tongue, all right!"

"A thousand pardons. That black horse, it surprised me to see it here. It once belonged to me."

"That's funny." Starr relaxed. "We found it down the wash, along with that sorrel. In the brush. I might trade it to you for the palomino."

Don Ricardo made a noncommittal gesture. "Did you find the rider?" His eyes were darting everywhere.

"No. We searched all over. Whiskers claims he never saw it or the sorrel before. Says they must've strayed there off the desert. I dunno, maybe they did." Starr turned away, saying over his shoulder, "Guess you'll want to eat." His men squatted down on their heels again, watching the Mexicans dismount and off-saddle.

The two outfits didn't fraternize a bit. Expediency had brought them into setting up a trading arrangement in their horse-stealing operations. Friendship was no part of it. They were alien to each other. Two such widely dissimilar individuals as Gooseneck Starr and Don Ricardo de Risa couldn't be expected to jog in harmony, except for brief business encounters.

While his men tended to their horses and cooked a meal, Don Ricardo strolled restlessly about the ghost town, poking into ruined buildings, pausing every so often to frown at the black horse. He swept searching glances all over the wide ledge, as if to catch a glimpse of something that kept eluding him.

"He knows I'm somewhere near him," Bishop muttered. "It makes him edgy."

"Just because of your horse?" McLean asked. "It could've changed hands since you got it from him, for all he knows."

Bishop shook his head. "The horse got him started. Now he's felt me watching him. He's the kind who senses things, like some wild animals do—and like some men who've been hunted for a long time. Roone knows what I mean."

"Yeah," Roone said. "When you're stalkin' a man, you try to keep your mind off him. Injuns do it when they're out to capture wild horses. You put your mind on him too strong, Bishop!"

"Right, I did. He doesn't have to see me, to know I'm around."

"You an' him must know each other pretty good," Roone observed acutely.

"We've met a few times," Bishop allowed, letting the bare statement take the weight of numerous encounters. He and Don Ricardo had crossed trails more than a few times, ridden together, clashed, and left scars. They had outwitted and tricked each other to the hilt on occasion, to the mutually unforgivable extent where trickery and double-cross merged in a single track.

He watched Don Ricardo wander to Russian Jack's signal fire on the rim, now dying out. Don Ricardo stood there for a moment fingering his chin, head bent in thought. He suddenly stooped over to touch the ground,

63

and Bishop knew that he had spotted the gouge made by the bullet from the muzzle-loader, when Tandra had fired close at McLean's feet. Moving on closer to the rim, Don Ricardo touched the ground again. He wiped his finger with a handkerchief, while examining a second bullet scar in the rock.

Roone leaned cautiously over and said in Bishop's ear, "That's blood from my arm! Look, he's figgerin' the angle them two bullets came from. That Mexican's too smart!"

VIII

BISHOP COMPRESSED his wide mouth. "He's sharp as a razor. That's what keeps him alive. Watch him work it out!" From an impartial and detached viewpoint it was intriguing to note his old enemy's mental processes.

Meantime his nose caught the aroma of coffee. Mexican coffee. Sweet as love, as the saying went, black as sin, and hot as hell. And frijoles with chili. His stomach growled.

Don Ricardo cocked his head, gazing speculatively at the two bullet scars in the rock. The pitch of their leaden smears couldn't fail to tell him that the shots had been fired from a high level. He swung around and raised his eyes until he was looking directly up at the great arched back of Bronco Rock, at the shadowed indentation above it.

Screened by the cedar clump and the shadow, Bishop didn't move a muscle, neither did McLean, but Roone drew back, whispering, "The son-'va-bitch is onto us!"

"He saw you move, damn you!" McLean breathed.

Don Ricardo quirked an eyebrow. He ran his glance downward to the cabin and inspected its construction,

64

flush against the cliff. Smiling, he sauntered toward it, nodding affably to Starr and his men as he passed them. He stopped by the black horse to scratch its left cheek and speak to it in Spanish. The horse pricked its ears forward interestedly at him; it normally didn't much care for familiarities.

He raised his head and smiled up at Bronco Rock, deliberately, knowingly. Walking on to the cabin, he yawned, and called to his men to wake him up in half an hour. He entered the cabin, closing the door after him.

Bishop eased back from the cedar clump. He faced the stope and drew his guns. It wouldn't take Don Ricardo long to discover the two loose planks. While waiting, Bishop recalled the various occasions when he had managed to put the don in a jackpot. It was like Don Ricardo to come exploring alone, to give himself the satisfaction of paying off old scores singlehanded. This was his day. He would make the most of it.

A light tread presently sounded in the stope. Don Ricardo stepped up into the cave. His white teeth flashed in a wide smile at sight of Bishop.

"*Viejo compadre!* What a happy surprise, Rogue! When I saw my black horse—"

"*My* horse, Rico! By trade, remember?"

"How well I remember! The buckskin you left me was a locoed goat, and its saddle pockets were filled with stones instead of money. I had a devil of a time getting out of Texas." Don Ricardo blandly ignored Bishop's drawn guns. His sparkling gaze darted rapidly over McLean and Roone, to Tandra.

He caught his breath. He doffed his sombrero and bowed. "You have company, Rogue. Excuse my intrusion."

"Make yourself at home. Stay for breakfast."

"Thank you, no." He had not missed noticing the scarcity of food in the cave. "My men are preparing mine.

65

Hot frijoles and chili, young beef, good Mexican coffee—"

"Shut up!" snarled Roone.

"You are hungry? Then join me. I insist." Don Ricardo's gaze stayed on Tandra. His eyes glowed appreciatively. He was highly susceptible to young and pretty women, and none too particular in his methods of pursuing them. "I insist!" he repeated softly.

"I insist we don't!" Bishop said, and the don then flicked a look at his guns.

"You offer a noisy argument! It would bring up all the men from below. No, Rogue, you are not in a position to argue with me. A shot would betray you."

"I might quietly dent your skull with a gunbarrel!"

"Not a good thing to try!" Don Ricardo kept a prudent distance. He rested his hands on his gun butts, and in an abrupt change of manner he dropped the mocking politeness and became the hard-bitten desperado. "Put away your guns, Rogue, you can't bluff me! You've got yourself bottled up tight!"

Even his speech changed, the words blunt, the touch of accent more pronounced.

"How you got into this fix, I don't know, but—*bueno hay!* It's my chance to pay you off, friend Rogue."

"If you're going to spill on us," Bishop said, "I might's well shoot you now and be done with it!"

"Wait!" McLean interceded. "Would he tell Starr we're up here, spying on him? Just for a grudge?"

"There was a time when he wouldn't," Bishop replied, looking bleakly at Don Ricardo. "If you can believe it, he was once a pretty good hombre, a caballero. Rode with the best, the kind that always gave the other man an even break, and never let a *compadre* down. But the best of 'em do change. I guess maybe he would."

"If you force me to, yes. I hold it over your head, while you dance to my tune!" Don Ricardo chuckled grimly. "Who is this girl?"

"Russian Jack's granddaughter, Tandra," Bishop said,

taking no pleasure in the introduction. "That's McLean, and the other's Roone."

"Russian Jack? Who—"

"You call him Whiskers."

"*Bien, bien,* the wily old one! He kept her hidden up here from us, eh? A rose unseen, wasting her sweetness in a dismal cave! This can't go on. Tandra? A pretty name. I shall enjoy your company at breakfast!"

McLean started forward. Bishop blocked him, and demanded, "What're you saying, Rico? She can't go down there!"

"She can, under my protection," retorted Don Ricardo, "and she will!"

"She will not!" snapped McLean. "I'll see you in hell first!"

"You'll see hell here, if she doesn't! You can't stand a siege by Starr and his crew. You would starve, or die of thirst. She would die with you. I am offering you your lives."

"At a price!" Bishop said.

"She is the price," Don Ricardo agreed. He smiled maliciously. "Rogue, you are right. We do change. You will feel changed after buying your life at the cost of a woman, eh? What a joke—Rogue Bishop hiding behind skirts! You will never be the same again!"

He bowed to Tandra, his gaze warm. "We will tell Starr that I brought you along in my pocket. It should puzzle that long-necked ape! You are coming?"

"No!"

"You need a little time to overcome your shyness. Perhaps a little persuasion. Gentlemen, I shall expect you to send her down in about half an hour!" Don Ricardo descended into the stope, smiling back at Bishop. "I hope you have no trouble reaching your decision."

Bishop glared balefully after him. For the first time he regretted pulling a switch on the don in Texas and rooking him out of his champion horse. On afterthought, he didn't. There had been grounds for grudges between them before that. The game, as they played it, was cutthroat and conscienceless, each of them seizing any possible advantage over the other. About the only scruple left was the one that disapproved of a bullet in the back, and that was a lingering tribute to the punctilious scruples of other days. Those days were not so very far back, in terms of years, but the golden brotherhood had lived fast and burned out. Its young-old relics were tending bar, or on the long dodge, gone bad. The new crop was grubby by contrast, like Starr and his crew.

Rico had him cornered. His offer of a shabby trade was designed to humble him. It didn't hold any guarantee against further acts of revenge. Rico's sense of humor was wickedly prankish.

Bishop looked at McLean, who watched him, trying to read his intentions. He shook his head, and McLean did the same. Catching the exchange, Roone put in a vote of protest.

"Don't be fools! She's got to go down to the Mexican! We're dead ducks if we don't play along with him!"

McLean brought the butt of his rifle up within inches of Roone's face. "Quiet, you self-loving scum!"

Bishop eased low to the mouth of the cave and peered down. He saw Don Ricardo emerge from the cabin below, slapping dust from his clothes. The don raised his head, turning, and gazed upward as though studying Bronco Rock. With a thumb he smoothed his thin mustache, by exaggeration making of it a purposeful gesture of self-satisfaction, knowing Bishop watched him.

Also watching him was Russian Jack, standing in the street. He had seen him leave the cabin. He followed the direction of the don's gaze, and Bishop saw the old man's black eyes widen. Don Ricardo strolled on to his men and stood at a cookfire, rocking contentedly on his heels and smiling to himself. The men joked with him, asking what he had dreamed of to make him so lighthearted. They suggested several colorful dreams involving women.

"Wait, *guerreros míos*," Bishop heard him reply, laughing. "Wait and I shall show you my dream!"

Guerreros. They were of the breed, all right. Chaparral warriors.

"I ain't going to wait here to die!" Roone declared. "You can do as you like, but I aim to get out!"

"You'll stay where you are," Bishop told him. "If one of us tries a break-out on his own, it'll give away the rest."

"How about the Mexican? He'll blow his gaff when the girl don't go down to him!"

"We'll ride the chance he won't. You sit tight."

"It's my life!"

"A lousy life!" McLean commented. "How does a man get to be like you?"

Roone eyed him. "You Southerners, with your fancy manners!" he sneered. "Plantation gentry. I hate your kind!"

"Gentry? Me?" McLean grinned. "I was raised on a tobacco farm. Not a plantation. A farm. I worked in the fields before I went to school. I've gone hungry many a time since."

"You wasn't born in a city slum. You didn't grow up not knowin' who spawned you. I swore I'd get out o' St. Louis and make money somehow." Roone struck his knee with his fist. "And I did! I had to scrabble for pennies, beg at back doors for folk's leavin's, and live like a homeless cur. But I made it! I got out o' there an' left all the stink behind me. I don't drink, smoke, or cuss, and I stay on the side o' the law."

McLean moved away from him, revolted by a self-righteous nature that bragged of paltry virtues while not boggling at manslaughter for profit. "I guess you learned to hate as a kid."

"Sure I did!"

"It's stayed with you. That's one part of the stink you didn't leave behind."

A commotion broke out below. McLean crouched beside Bishop for a view of what was happening. "My God!" he exclaimed. "The old man's gone mad!"

Russian Jack, carrying a gunpowder keg on his left shoulder, was running lumberingly toward the cookfires. A stub of fuse protruding from the keg gave off a trickle of blue smoke. As he ran, the heavy keg wobbled precariously on his shoulder, and he reached up with his silver hook to steady it. His frenzied eyes were fastened on Don Ricardo.

The men were on their feet, staring in amazement. They had come to take for granted that Russian Jack was an addled old hermit, harmless, and were unaware of any reason why he should launch himself as a living bomb. But his object was plain. He packed enough gunpowder to annihilate Don Ricardo and everybody else within range of the blast, as well as himself.

There was a rush, men following their first instinct to bolt for cover. Starr collided with two of his crew and stepped into a fire, kicking over a coffee pot. He issued from a cloud of steam, tugging at a scalding wet leg of his pants.

Taking a wrestler's half-crouch, arms bent forward and hands open, Don Ricardo watched Russian Jack come at him. A bullet would not dispose of the fused keg, now too close for him to excape its explosion. He would wrestle for it rather than run. In size his slim build was dwarfed by that of Russian Jack, but Bishop had known him to outwrestle brawny young Indian bucks.

Enraged by his accident with the hot coffee, Starr bellowed, "Shoot him, you goddam Mexican clown!"

"No, you long-necked *animalucho!*" Don Ricardo snapped back, setting his balance for a leap at the keg.

Starr pulled out a gun, took aim, and fired.

Russian Jack stumbled two steps. His knees buckled and he fell forward. He thrust at the keg, rolling it on at Don Ricardo.

The don darted at it, blocked it with his foot, and quickly plucked out the burning fuse and stamped on it. He wiped his face before putting on an expression of amused condescension for all those who had scattered, but his eyes narrowed when he looked at Starr.

"Your bullet could have got me blown to pieces! His fall might easily have jolted the fuse on into the keg and exploded it. I said not to shoot him!"

"You was makin' a big play," Starr jeered. He walked to Russian Jack and stared down at him. "Wonder what got into the old cuss?"

"Leave him alone."

"Why should I? He needs another bullet."

IX

TANDRA WAS CRYING, huddled close to McLean. "Grandy! My poor Grandy!"

Bishop looked around at her. "If that powder keg had gone off—" he began, and didn't finish the sentence. "Where's Roone?"

McLean crawled back and peered into the stope. "He's gone. Left while our backs were turned. I'm going after him."

"Hurry! If he tries a break-out, we're finished." Bishop kept watch on the cabin below.

Roone appeared, easing slowly from the door. He went unnoticed in the aftermath of the disturbance. The men were drifting back to the cookfires, talking of Russian Jack's mad outburst, wagging their heads. Roone made for the head of the old wagon road, his iron nerve hold-

71

ing him to a casual and unhurried pace, his back toward the men. Years as a man hunter had trained him in the use of deceptive naturalness.

He was close to the wagon road, when Starr, taking his eyes off Don Ricardo, said, "Who's that feller?"

"It's Shorty Summers."

"The hell it is. I'm right here."

"Then who—"

"Hey, you!" Starr called out.

Roone kept to the same pace. He raised a hand, not turning his head, and waggled it in sign that he had heard Starr's hail. As he started down the wagon road he slapped his backside, then dropped from sight. Some of the men gave nods of understanding, but Starr continued frowning, undecided.

"Who's missin'?"

It took a minute to ascertain that none of those present could state with certainty if anybody was missing.

"Hold still while I count up." Starr counted heads. "We're all here! Get after that feller!"

"Where'd he come from? We searched—"

"Get after him!" He led a race to the wagon road. "Dammit, I knew spies was up here! I'll roast that old cuss alive!"

A horse went tearing down from the holding grounds below the other end of the ledge. Once out of sight, Roone had moved fast to get himself a mount. From the cave, Bishop saw him riding bareback, plunging down the slopes. At that headlong gait he would either break his neck or make his getaway. Shots cracked after him. He flattened out on the horse, slapping it with his hat. The horse went wild, taking the slopes in sliding leaps and squealing its fright.

McLean came up out of the stope. "Roone left the planks hanging open," he said. "The Judas! I've shut them. Did he get clear away?"

Bishop nodded, moving back from the mouth of the

cave. "He's light, no saddle weight, and he got hold of a good horse. I doubt they'll waste time trying to catch him. He's the kind that makes it when others don't."

"So he'll head for Wickenburg to get help from his cattlemen bosses."

"Not for us! We're in his black book."

Starr could be heard bellowing at his crew to search again the ghost town and old mine workings. One of the men called a caustic remark about locking the stable after the horse was gone. Others sang out that a sand storm was rising in the south, that they ought to move out ahead of it, not waste time. Starr shouted them down.

"We don't risk buckin' no sandstorm with a horse herd! We stay here till it blows over. If it's a ripper it'll perish that feller. He ain't got no water. There's another spy hidin' where he was. Find him! I'll work on Whiskers. The fire'll make him talk up!"

Bishop looked at McLean. "Damn your silver!"

McLean nodded somberly. "Hell can have it. If Roone—"

"Forget Roone. He looks out for himself. He might make it to Wickenburg. If he could get back here in time with a posse—which he can't—he'd line us up for the kill. Or take us in and swear our lives away. I'd as soon argue with Starr, or Rico. Or both."

"I guess we don't have much chance."

"None I'd bet on."

"I've wondered sometimes," McLean said, "if there's a curse on that kind of treasure. Something always happens just when you think you've got it. I wish my father had burned Sandy Mac's letter."

"You sound cured."

"I am. Too late. The *contrabando* raiders—all killed except Russian Jack. The silver brought us here, and now it's us. And Tandra. What's going to happen to her? We got her into this. Because of the silver. The cursed silver! How do we get her out?"

73

To Bishop the line of reasoning wasn't altogether straight. Between wealth and the actual possession of it lay rocky roads, often studded with pitfalls, otherwise everybody would get rich. Treasure needed no curse to protect it. As for Tandra, she had been brought here by Russian Jack. Some day her situation was bound to have become desperate. The old raider couldn't expect to live forever, guarding her. For that matter, it had become a toss-up which of the two was guarding the other.

"How do we get her out? How?"

Bishop didn't reply, listening to light feet hurriedly mounting the stope, spurs jingling. A solution existed, one which he guessed occurred to McLean, for the younger man turned white. They both avoided looking at Tandra.

Don Ricardo ascended to the top step. He nodded to Bishop and McLean. "A pity you let the little lawman slip out. It makes a bad business. *Ay*, very bad!"

"What was good about it before?" Bishop queried.

"Well, at least I would not have exposed your hideout to Starr."

"You threatened to!"

"Only to remind you I had the upper hand. A pleasure to myself. I am about to lose that pleasure." Don Ricardo spoke to Tandra. "Your grandfather—"

"Has he—died?"

"No, unfortunately. Starr is positive he hid two law spies, and that one is still in hiding. He's preparing to hang him over the fire until he talks."

The girl shuddered. "No! Oh, no!"

Don Ricardo spread his hands. "I regret it, myself." He turned back to Bishop. "Who can say how long the old man can bear that torture? Meantime, Starr's men search everywhere. Your hideout is certain to be discovered soon. They'll smoke you out, and that will be the end of it."

"Thanks for your sympathy, Rico!"

"Sympathy for you? I have none to spare on you, Rogue. My sympathy goes to Tandra and her grandfather, if you force them to suffer. The old man will die a horrible death. If Tandra stays here with you and McLean what will her end be? At best, a bullet. You and McLean are sacrificing them! Sacrificing them on the hopeless chance of saving yourselves!"

Bishop breathed hard, staring at the don, picking over what he had said and trying to determine whether the words were genuine or guileful. "What answer have you got?" he demanded.

"Let Tandra go with me! I can save her and the old man. That's more than you can do!" Don Ricardo stood straight and taut, dark eyes accusing. "You said I was once 'a pretty good hombre,' and I said we change. Now I say you've changed more than I have!"

Bishop raised a hand as if to strike him in the face. "You and Starr are close on the outs. He'd take her away from you!"

The don didn't flinch a muscle. "Not while I live! I don't have enough men to fight Starr's crew, but he wouldn't want a showdown with me!" He flicked a quick glance to Tandra. "And the wounded old man wouldn't die hanging head-down over a fire!"

Tandra pulled away from McLean, whispering, "I must! I must go with him, don't you see? For Grandy's sake, I—"

"Wait!" Bishop waved her back. "Rico, when you found me here you sort of wondered what it was that could've brought me to this place, didn't you? Finding me here surprised you."

"Not for long. The hazards of travel in this hellish country can drive any man to take shelter for a spell. Sandstorms. Lack of water." Don Ricardo shrugged. "When Starr and his riders showed up, you wisely kept

75

out of sight. They'd kill anybody to keep this rendezvous from being discovered."

"No, you're only part right. I came here with Mc-Lean on the track of a fortune. *Contrabando* silver, a big mule-train of it, captured years ago by a gang of raiders headed by Russian Jack. We haven't had much chance to search, but we know it's cached here. I've got an idea where it is, too. Half of it's mine. I'll peddle it to you!"

"What are you buying?"

"You and your *guerreros!* Stand with us against the Starr bunch, and you can have my half of the silver."

"And mine!" McLean said.

"Your generosity overwhelms me!" Don Ricardo murmured. He eyed Bishop with cynical admiration. "I recall the locoed buckskin and the stone-filled saddle pockets. And two or three other occasions when you dazzled me into chasing rainbows for pots of gold, while you picked up the winnings! This time it is silver. Mere silver. But an enormous cache, of course. *Ay*, I know you too well!" He wagged his head. "What a rogue you are, Rogue!"

Bishop pulled out Sandy Mac's letter, creased and frayed. "Read this."

"Sorry, there isn't time. Any minute now they may stumble onto this hideout, and it would embarrass me to be found in it with you. Starr is fixing a tripod over the fire for the old man. Tandra? Stay here and listen to his screams, or come with me and save him! Which is it?"

"I—I—yes, I'm coming!" Tandra stammered. She shook her head hopelessly at McLean. "Please don't try to stop me."

Bishop crushed an urge to match draws with the don and have it out. It would gain nothing to kill and be killed. "Leave her here, Rico! Leave her here and do what you can for Russian Jack, and—"

76

"And you'll make me rich, eh? Another rainbow!"

"There's no trick about the silver. It's here! On my oath!"

Don Ricardo raised an eyebrow. "You make it sound so convincing I would incline to believe it, if you were anyone else. Those stone-filled saddle pockets—no, no, never again! I would believe you only if you showed me the silver. Can you?"

"Not now. Later on."

"*Muy bien!* Let's make a bargain. When I start back south, which will be soon, I shall go by way of Yellow Wells and on past Tonopah down to Agua Caliente, then to—"

"I know the route."

"Tandra will be my guest. My treasured, unharmed guest."

"Unharmed?" McLean broke in.

"That is what I said, and my word is good."

"What's the bargain?" Bishop asked.

"You have sworn that the silver is real, no tricks. I take your word for it." Don Ricardo's tone dripped utter disbelief. His eyes brightly mocked Bishop. "If you catch up with me before I reach Mexico, I'll trade you Tandra for the silver! That is a fair bargain, no?"

"No!" Bishop said. "How do I trail you, with Starr's mob blocking me in this hole?"

"That," murmured Don Ricardo, "is one of your problems!" He steered Tandra to the stope, his hand under her arm. "Only one of them. There will be others." They descended the stope together, he quietly humming, she trembling.

Bishop glanced at McLean's haggard face, and went to the lookout behind the scrub cedar, speculating as to how Rico would go about escorting Tandra safely past Starr and out onto his route to Mexico. There was certain to be some stiff opposition to that. Starr's men were wrecking the ghost town, surging in groups from one place to the next, busily searching for a hidden spy. Not the dimmest chance of spiriting the girl out unseen

Bishop shook his head. That was one of Rico's problems.

X

USHERING TANDRA out of the cabin, chatting lightly to her as if promenading a plaza, Don Ricardo made no effort whatever to escape the notice of Starr and his searching men. He smiled and nodded to his *guerreros*, took Tandra's hand in his, and rolled Russian Jack's powder keg out of her path with his foot.

"What the—!" Starr's voice was muffled for once, choked with astonishment. "Where in hell did you get *her?*"

Don Ricardo plucked a cigarette from a gold case, a piece of battered finery left over from some period of high affluence in his career. "Your language, in the hearing of a young lady, is deplorably coarse!" he reproved.

Starr stalked up to him. His men came running, raising a babble of amazed questions. "Where'd you get her, Risa? Where?"

"What matters? Never question a gift from the gods. I have promised her that she will gather flowers in the floating gardens of Río Lerma, view Popocatépetl by moonlight, join in the gay life of—"

"You found her hidin' here!" Starr cut off the don's flight of airy anticipation. Tandra broke away from the don. Starr grabbed at her. She eluded him and ran to Russian Jack, lying near the fire. Starr stared after her. His eyes shrank to crinkled slits. "Who is she?"

"The old man's granddaughter. She is under my protection, so leave her alone."

"Oh? You take too goddam much on y'self, Risa! She's as much mine as yours! We share this rendezvous, don't we?"

The *guerreros* gathered silently behind the don, stiff faces masking their worry. Though badly outnumbered, they would fight, given the word. They were of the *hombres del campo* breed. But it would be a lost fight. Starr's men, lining up with him, stared at them stonily.

Don Ricardo blew a thin spear of cigarette smoke, outwardly cool and at ease. "That is true," he admitted reflectively. "Loot law, eh? Yes, plunder must be shared. All plunder. One must never hold out on a *compadre*. You are right, Starr, she is as much yours as mine!"

McLean slid his rifle forward and sighted along it. Bishop reached to it quickly and pushed it aside.

"Not yet!"

"Good thing you seen the light, Risa!" Starr at once started for the girl.

Don Ricardo let him go three strides, and said, "Before you take her, *compadre*, let me confess that there is other loot here for us to share! I was tempted to keep it to myself, but"—he shrugged—"you showed me the light. There is plenty enough to go around. We'll not fight over it."

Starr swung back to him. "What other loot?"

"Silver," Don Ricardo replied. "A big mule-train load of it! I learned of it when I found the girl. Russian Jack has it cached up here. Great stacks of pure silver," he went on, inspired, "as high as your head! Tons! It—"

"Where?" The shout came not only from Starr, but from most of his crew.

"Here's where we get it!" Bishop muttered. "Don't shoot at him! Let him pull it off."

"Why?" McLean challenged him.

"He's got to get them occupied, to give him time to get away with the girl." Bishop's voice was flat. "He's got to do it."

Don Ricardo took a drag at his cigarette, cutting a glance upward. He nodded toward the cabin. "In the back wall of that cabin there are two loose planks, and behind them is an old mine tunnel that—"

He had no need to add any further details. Starr led the rush, his crew crowding on his heels. The greed on their faces verged upon rabid lust, causing McLean to blurt, "My God, did I ever look like that?"

"You did," Bishop told him. "Gold fever, silver fever, it does that to most of us." He drew his guns and tipped their muzzles at the stope, waiting, conjecturing on what Rico would do next to prolong the diversion. Rico wouldn't abandon the stolen horses; he couldn't afford to leave any horses behind to mount a pursuit. He had to gain time to organize a getaway.

A faint bang told of the two loose planks being slammed open, followed by an increasing sound of feet stumbling in darkness, of voices calling for matches. Bishop waited for the oncoming commotion to advance to the foot of the stope. He fired a single shot that momentarily stilled the noise.

"That goddam Risa!" Starr swore. "He didn't say nothin' about somebody guardin' the silver!"

One of the men, less muddled by visions of fortune, inquired, "If it's guarded, how'd Risa get to see it? Maybe he was lying!"

"What for?"

"Just to get a laugh on us. You know how he is. Maybe there ain't no silver." Sudden urgency edged the speaker's voice. "Y'ask me, we oughta go back an' see what he's up to! He's full o' tricks."

That man, Bishop decided, was too shrewdly suspicious. Others, swayed by his skepticism, began agreeing with him that Don Ricardo had most likely fooled them, that there wasn't any hoard of silver in the abandoned old mine. Starr argued against them in a tone of dwindling conviction. There was a hidden spy, they granted.

It wouldn't take all of them to smoke him out. They were in favor of splitting the bunch, half of them to go back.

They were apt to upset Rico's design, a design that was the lesser of two evils. Loudly Bishop said to McLean, "They can only come up one at a time, and these bags of silver make us a good barricade!"

McLean looked at him. "That'll bring them!"

"It should!"

Starr shouted, "You hear that?" His guns blazed ahead of a rushing advance up the hewn steps of the stope.

Bullets ricocheted off the curved roof of the cave, and Bishop stooped low, brushing a flying chip of rock from his neck. His loud mention of silver, meant to delay Starr's men from quitting the mine, was more effective than he anticipated. It made believers of the skeptics. The lure of treasure brought them scrambling up the narrow stope in a close-packed mass, those in the forefront forced onward by the pressure from behind.

The first one of them reared up, practically borne aloft. It wasn't Starr. McLean's rifle spurted, and Bishop checked his trigger-squeeze and saved a shell. The man tumbled back. There came sounds of scuffling, and Starr yelled, "Quit shovin', goddam you, the silver'll keep!"

He evidently managed to impose some degree of restraint on his men, for the pushing scramble slackened. A gun poked up and fired blindly at random into the cave. McLean uttered a grunt. Bishop placed a shot that knocked the gun away, and spoke without looking around.

"Did it get you?"

"Clipped me in the shoulder. My arm's numb." McLean tore his shirt open. "Dead numb."

"Work your rifle with one hand, then."

A heavy explosion shuddered the cave and shook down fragments of stone. Into its beginning echoes briefly in-

81

truded a crackle of collapsing mine timbers, followed by the prolonged, grinding rumble of falling rock. The echoes boomed out over the empty desert and faded off like rolling thunder, but for a while longer the underground rocks pounded until the last of them settled.

"The powder keg! De Risa's blown the tunnel in!" McLean spoke in a whisper of stunned dismay. The shock of the blast held the Starr men motionless in the stope, dumbfounded. "My God, he's sealed up the lot of us!"

"He had to do it," Bishop said somberly.

"But it—it's an inhuman trick!"

"Not to Rico. He knows I'd do it, given the same choice."

"Then you're inhuman too!" McLean snapped. "Your damned feud with him makes hellhounds of you both!"

Bishop let it pass, indifferent to anyone's opinion of him. A man's own opinion of himself was what mattered. McLean, desperately anxious over the girl, was forgetting that she could have fallen into Starr's hands if Rico hadn't blown up the tunnel. The feud played no special part in the motive for that ruthless stroke. Rico would have felt justified in doing it regardless of who got caught in the trap besides Starr and his crew.

You feel you gotta do a thing, you do it . . . but there's a lot o' folks don't savvy.

The rush of air from the explosion found its way to the only exit. Dust puffed from the stope like smoke from a gunbarrel. It galvanized the men caught in it. They came swarming up, choking, frantic. Firing through the haze, Bishop loosened a three-man jam at the top and drove them back.

"We can't hold them there!" McLean with one hand worked a fresh shell into the breech of his rifle. "They'd choke to death."

Starr, between coughing and sneezing, roared, "Let us out o' here!"

82

"You can come up one at a time," Bishop answered. "No guns, and hands high!"

"To hell with that!"

"Then stay there! The dust'll soon thin out."

They cursed, huddling on the steps. The rush of air ceased, the dust settled, and they held a mumbling conference. In the lull, Don Ricardo called up from outside, "*Qué paso, Rogue?*"

"Much you care, you blasted twister!" Bishop returned, reloading his guns. "You pulling out now?"

"There's nothing more to keep me here. Tell Starr for me that our business partnership is finished. I'm taking all the horses."

"My black too?"

"*My* black! Anyway, you can't use it up there. And I don't know how you can get down, unless you sprout wings." Don Ricardo chuckled, treating the thing as a prank. The chuckle sounded a trifle forced. "What a predicament!"

"That's a fact," Bishop observed to McLean. He raised his voice again. "If that sandstorm catches you in the open, you're liable to lose every head."

"I must risk it. This place is unhealthy." But still the don lingered. "Tandra—" he began, and paused. "I don't expect you to catch up with us!"

"Then you lose out on the silver."

"Ah, that miraculous silver! You go on dangling rich bait, trying somehow to hook me, but your bait is a mirage! You never give up, do you? Not to your last breath. Starr and his *animaluchos* will find that out!" Don Ricardo was silent for a moment. Then he barked abruptly, "*Adiós, Rogue!*"

"S'long, Rico!"

McLean looked out from the cave. "There he goes, damn him, with Tandra! She's looking back, crying." He bowed his head, eyes shut tight. "They're gone . . ."

The *guerreros* raised high-pitched yells, starting the

drive. The hoofbeats of the double herd of horses thundered down the old wagon road. The noise changed pitch as the desert sand was reached, becoming a muffled drumming, rapidly decreasing in the distance.

McLean lifted his head and stared around blindly at Bishop. "He took Tandra and left us here to die—yet you talked almost like a couple of fellows jawing over a horse race!" He clenched his fist. "Like it was some kind of a game just between you two, and who else got hurt wasn't important!"

Bishop frowned, recognizing some truth in the charge. "Rico's a double-crossing cuss," he granted, "but he kept the girl from getting hurt by Starr. He left us here mainly to hold the bunch back—"

"While he carries her off to Mexico! Are you excusing him for it?"

"No," Bishop said, boggling at the thought of excusing his old enemy for putting him in a jackpot. Nobody would be more surprised than Rico. "He knows I'll pay him off if I get out of this fix."

McLean made a harsh sound in his throat. "There it is! Just you two, and to hell with anybody else! You'd—"

"Save it! They're coming up again!"

Starr and his men, having finished a frustrating conference and examined their problem from every angle, could find no better solution than to stage another rush. But they added an improvement. Handicapped by the narrowness of the stope, they elected one of their number to lead them as an unwilling shield, and propelled him bodily upward.

The unlucky individual was stout. He wobbled wildly, firing two guns, men down behind launching him on. It was McLean, using his rifle with one arm, who promptly shot him. Bishop, closer to the stope, was trying for the hoisters below, preferably Starr himself.

The stout man toppled back. His dead weight sank on the men who were half carrying him, and in the restricted space not enough hands could reach to hold him up. They gave way, stumbling on the roughly chiseled stone steps into those below. Bishop took the opportunity to pitch three shots into the stope, adding to the close-packed confusion.

It would, he hoped, discourage further attacks for a while. His supply of shells was limited, and McLean had few spares for his rifle, if any. The shells could buy time and that was all.

"Bishop!" McLean said. "The old man's gone and got a rope. He's coming back with it."

"So?" Bishop changed his position, watching the stope for developments. "What good's a rope down there to us?"

"He seems to know what he's doing, but he looks nearly dead. Can hardly stay on his feet."

"That's what I mean. He's got a bullet in him."

"All the same, I think he's about to try throwing the rope up to me," McLean said. "He knows what's happened. He saw de Risa take Tandra off with him. If he could get us down out of here—"

"What kind of rope's he got?"

"An old derrick rope, I'd say. Dry and stiff, by the way he handles it."

A feeling of pessimism pressed on Bishop. "Couldn't throw it in a well!" he grunted.

XI

SWAYING IN HIS bloodstained rags, Russian Jack halted and gazed upward, his gaunt face grimly calm, sunken black eyes measuring the distance. He held the old rope looped in his one hand and over his wrist and forearm. With his silver hook he carefully arranged the loops so that they wouldn't run together and kink. That done, he nodded up to McLean, who leaned out watching him.

"Ready!" McLean called. But to Bishop he muttered, "He can't do it!"

Russian Jack took stance, sideways to the cave, legs apart. He spread his bony shoulders and arms, stood motionless as if commanding by will power the return of his once mighty strength, and hurled the rope with a sudden twist of his body.

The rope uncoiled higher and higher. Its knotted end slapped rock a yard short of its goal, and it fell in a tangle onto the remains of the cabin, which the explosion had wrecked. McLean, reaching out empty-handed, groaned. That wounded old giant had put all he had into the throw, spent his strength for nothing, and couldn't possibly do better.

Laboriously Russian Jack gathered up the fallen rope. It was balky, stiff in places, frayed in others, a dead rope without any springy give to it. He straightened out its kinks, doggedly refusing defeat, and coiled it on the ground. Searching about, he chose a piece of rock. He sank to his knees heavily and fumbled for a long time with the rock and the rope.

Listening to the Starr men sort themselves out, Bishop asked McLean, "What's he doing?"

"Tying a rock onto it," McLean answered. "Not easy for him, only one hand and a hook. There, he's done it. Lord," he breathed, "give him strength!"

The old man pushed himself up onto his feet, the tied rock dangling from his hand. Maddeningly deliberate, he began to swing the rock in a widening arc, paying out more rope. He teetered and lost control, and the rope wrapped around him. He slowly unwound it and began once more, his eyes turned upward to the cave, his feet planted wide, knees bent.

At last, with a final strain that left him staggering to

a sprawl, he let it go. The slung piece of rock, the rope snaking behind it, smashed through the cedar fringe. Reaching far out with his good arm, McLean caught it. His numbed arm let him down and he overbalanced, sliding head-first into the cedars. He gave out a yell.

Bishop looked around. He jumped, grabbed McLean by the ankles, and hauled him back. The sight of the rope swept away his pessimism. "*Bueno!*" He briskly dragged it up. "Tie it round you. I'll lower you down. Don't forget your rifle."

"You could get shot in the back doing it," McLean objected, "and I'd get a fast drop!"

Bishop reached down and tied the rope to a cedar limb. "Don't argue! I'll be right after you. They'll be up in here soon's they know we're gone. I want you down there ready with your rifle, in case they try to pick me off while I'm coming down the rope."

"I might've known you were looking out for yourself!" said McLean, fastening the rope under his arms. He forced a grin. "And this old rope's none too safe. So I test it first, eh?"

"You're catching on."

"Okay, all set."

Bishop took a turn of the rope around his middle and clamped his elbow on it. Braced, he used one hand to pay it out, letting McLean's weight provide the pull. It made for a rapid and somewhat jerky descent, he guessed, but that couldn't be helped. He had to leave one hand free to hold a gun.

A sound of cautious movement came from the stope. The men there were suspecting that something was afoot. Bishop slanted a bullet at the stope and spoke aloud to nonexistent companions: "Good thing we brought in plenty shells, boys!"

Somebody backed down the stone steps, muttering in

87

reply to a query, "I dunno how many—didn't get a chance to look!"

"Bet it's a bluff!"

"You want to call it?"

The strain on the rope finally slackened, and McLean gave a tug as signal that he had reached bottom. Holstering the gun, Bishop threw the extra rope out and started down it hand-over-hand. It didn't give to his weight. He drew no sense of security from that. He was bigger and heavier than McLean.

McLean's rifle cracked below. Gunfire answered it. Starr and his crew had soon discovered that the cave contained neither silver nor men. McLean ran in closer to the cliff, rock chips spurting behind him, and fired again. The disadvantage of his numbed arm made his shooting less than accurate.

Bishop felt a slight jolt, and swiftly looked up. Two frayed strands of the rope hung loose. As he looked, a third strand parted. The rope stretched at that weakened spot, slowly unwinding, swinging him around. His weight had proved too much for it, or else McLean's hasty shot had clipped it. Another turn or two, and it would ravel out and break.

He dipped a glance below, estimated his chances of sliding down the rope before it broke, and decided they were bad. He was hanging level with the belly of Bronco Rock, a sheer drop beneath him, and the turning of the rope was gathering momentum. Below the belly, crumbled rock lay spilled in a steep slant, rubble of the wind and weather that over the centuries had sculptured the great stone horse in bas-relief. Between the rubble and the rounded under-belly there was a space, a crevice that offered a safe landing if he could get to it in the next few seconds.

McLean, noticing the broken strands, shouted, "Watch out, it's going!" Which made two holding the same opinion.

Bishop raised his feet high and thrust them hard at Bronco Rock, swinging himself far out. He lowered his long legs and swung back, under the belly. McLean gaped, watching, unable to see from where he stood what Bishop was aiming at. The added strain broke the rope and left him plunging at the crevice. He shot into it feet first, narrowly missing a jut of rock. To McLean it appeared that he vanished into the solid face of the cliff.

When Bishop crawled out, smeared with dirt, he still had hold of the broken length of rope. He looped it around the jut of rock and let himself down the rest of the way. One knee of his pants was torn. His coat had split at the back, and his boots were badly scuffed. He examined the broken end of the rope.

"Where did you get to?" McLean asked.

Bishop eyed him meditatively. "There's a hole up there. It's a lot deeper than it looked, and I hit every bump. If I thought you were a good one-handed shot with that rifle, I'd twist this rope round your neck! Your bullet cut it."

"Sorry!"

"H'm!"

The men up in the cave had ceased their firing, unable to sight Bishop and McLean under the bulge of Bronco Rock. Russian Jack sat with his back to the cliff, arms folded over his bloodied chest, gazing out at the desert. Bishop strode over to him.

"Can you travel?"

Russian Jack raised his head. "You know I can't. I am here to stay." He grimaced. "Buzzards will pick at my corpse, and coyotes will gnaw my bones! A sorry end for an officer of the Imperial Russian Army."

"We all have to die."

"A cheerless truism. And few of us may choose the manner and place of our dying. Mine began in battle at Zurich. I killed my general for ordering a retreat. He

89

was a favorite of the Tsar, and I had to flee, leaving everything behind. Everything. It ends here. The cursed silver! The wasted years of searching. And I never found it—I never found it!"

Bishop didn't have the time or inclination to listen to reminiscences of a misspent life. He said tersely, "We're going after Tandra."

"You have no horses."

"We've got legs."

Russian Jack returned his gaze to the desert. "It is coming closer, the sandstorm."

"I don't look for it to go away," Bishop said. He motioned upward. "Part of the rope's still up there. They can string their belts onto it, and their shirts, and climb down one at a time." He unholstered a gun, flipped it, held it out butt foremost. "D'you remember how to use one of these?"

"I remember quite well!" Russian Jack took it and thumbed the hammer back. "Six loads?"

"It's all I can spare."

"Six will do. If you ever find Tandra—if she . . ."

"Uh-huh." Their eyes met for an instant. "S'long. Let's go, McLean. Stay close to the cliff till we're in the clear, then we work down through the brush. Not the wagon road. They can see part of it."

"You lead on. I'll cover the cave." McLean brought his rifle up ready.

"Yeah, try hitting the rope again!"

"You holding that against me?"

"Well, I don't give you credit for it!"

They hugged the cliff to the western end of the ledge and dropped off. Following Bishop through the patchy brush, McLean asked, "What do you reckon they'll do when they find we're gone?"

"Not much of anything for a spell," Bishop answered. "The old man's holding 'em while we get a start. I gave him a gun." A shot rang out, and he said, "That's him."

"You don't miss a bet, do you?"

"I try not to."

"A crippled old man, dying, left with a gun to guard our backtrail." McLean shook his head. "Mighty tough."

"His granddaughter's alive, bound for a Mexican honeymoon," Bishop said, and McLean winced. "Quit if it's too tough for your stomach! I'm going after Rico."

"You and him! Doesn't anything else count?"

"Yes. The girl. If I get her away from him, you lose out!" Bishop's tone was harsh. "You'll lose her and the silver too!"

McLean stared. "My God, do you mean—?"

"I mean she'll need a man to take care of her. A grown man who can lift her over the rough spots."

"Like a father?"

"I'm not that old!" Bishop growled. He swung his head and regarded the younger man with brutal irony. "Rico's about my age. Would you say his interest in her is paternal?"

"No! But he's—well, he's—"

"He's a man. So am I."

McLean met his look. "You're alike in other ways too! Tandra is just a bone of contention between you—something to fight over, like loot. But she's a human being! She's a living, breathing girl!"

"I'm damn-well aware of that—so's Rico!"

XII

THE ADVANCING sandstorm wiped out the horizon and joined earth and sky together in a sullen red haze. Following the tracks of the horse herd, the two men trudged to meet it. The flat floor of the Harque Hala offered no shelter; it shimmered under the sun until it vanished into the oncoming wall of whirling, sand-laden winds.

Bishop wiped sweat from his forehead and quietly cursed the necessity for footwork. The high, tapered heels of his riding boots sank into loose sand at each step, putting a nagging strain on the leg muscles. McLean had the best of it with his low-heeled boots. Bishop glanced at him and saw that his face was haggard. His wounded shoulder was giving McLean trouble. The arm was losing some of its numbness, but it was a hanging weight that wrenched his shoulder as he walked.

"Stop a minute," Bishop told him, "and we'll rig up a sling for that arm. Not your bandanna—you'll want it to cover your face when the storm hits. Here, I'll tear a strip off your shirt."

"We're wasting time!" McLean muttered.

"A minute won't matter much. It's a long way yet to Yellow Wells." Bishop fashioned the sling, leaving McLean bereft of his shirttail.

"What's at Yellow Wells?"

"A relay station, abandoned by a stage line that went broke. Couple of buildings, horse pens, and maybe the wells haven't gone dry yet. Rico's got a lot of horses and not enough riders to handle 'em through the storm. I figure he'll call a halt there."

"S'pose he doesn't?"

"Then I'll track him to Tonopah, pick up a horse, and take the route on down into Mexico if I have to."

"And me!"

"You'd never make it," Bishop said bluntly. "I doubt you're going to make it to Yellow Wells. Alum water and a bullet have worn the edge off you."

"I'll get there!" vowed McLean, and they tramped on. He saw Bishop presently tie a handkerchief over his nose and mouth, road-agent style. "Hard to believe we're near the storm, the air's so still," he said.

Bishop tugged his hat down. "Builds up pressure ahead of it." He helped McLean tie on his bandanna. Hatless, McLean could do little toward shielding his eyes. A flight of twittering birds raced northward overhead. "It's a bad one, high and wide."

The vast front of the storm bore down upon the two men. It swallowed them in a booming roar of swirling cross-winds and pelting sand, staggering them, stinging the skin where exposed. McLean, unprepared for the wild force of the onslaught, stumbled to his knees. He got up quickly to keep sight of Bishop and plodded after him, trying to shield his eyes with his forearm.

Bishop kept going, head bent, concentrating on his sense of direction. The sun was a red blur, and all landmarks were blanked out completely. The first few minutes of a sandstorm were sometimes the worst; you shortened them a bit by pushing on through. Sometimes. Not always.

The hot, dry winds increased. Sand filled his clothes and coated his masking handkerchief. Breathing grew difficult. At last he had to stop for a respite. He squatted down, his back to the fierce blow, and turned up the collar of his coat. He shook out the handkerchief, blew his caked nostrils, and retied it on between breaths. McLean loomed unsteadily through the eye-smarting dust and sand, and sank beside him.

"You still think you can make it, treasure hunter?"

"I can try, gunslinger!"

They had to shout to make themselves heard.

"This storm'll take a while to blow itself out. It's getting worse." Bishop's stomach growled with hunger. That and his thirst, a more acute discomfort, disinclined him to charity. "You can't keep up with me—and damned if I'll lug you!"

"Didn't ask you!" McLean retorted. He wiped his streaming eyes. "It's my lookout if I fall behind."

No argument there. "You still got your pocket compass? Bear south and a notch west, and you'll strike Yellow Wells sooner or later." Bishop wouldn't have bet a dollar on the compass. He rose to his feet, shoulders

93

hunched against the storm. Something more needed to be said. "Most times I'd lend a hand—"

"I know."

"But there's the girl."

"And you're hell-bent on scoring off on de Risa. I don't know how you'll do it, him with his outfit. And you've only got one gun left."

Bishop had no clear idea, himself, of how he was to go about it. The essential thing was to catch up with Rico. As to what might happen then, he had to leave such matters to the future, depending on whatever circumstances that could be twisted to his advantage. Unfortunately Rico had a sharp eye for tricks, and possessed a talent of his own for springing deadly surprises. It was a fatal mistake ever to underestimate him.

"Be seeing you." Bishop raised a hand and let it fall. He headed on into the sandstorm without waiting to see if McLean was getting up to follow him.

When he looked back, later, he guessed he was alone, but there was no knowing whether McLean was only a few paces or half a mile behind. The winds had strengthened and were sweeping up scuds of fine gravel along with the sand. The sun and sky were gone, and it was dark enough to send chickens to their roosts if any chickens could have survived.

His rancor mounted in proportion to his thirst, hunger, and the soreness of his feet. It drove out any forbearance that he might have entertained regarding Don Ricardo's drastic solution to a pressing problem. Rico was a low-down Judas, a shifty son of Satan, a double-crossing horse thief. Shooting was too good for him.

"Like to get my hands round his neck!"

The storm abated at last, revealing nightfall. The tail-end of it passed on northward, the dust dissipated, and the air grew clear and still. Stars sparkled in a black velvet sky, the moon not yet risen. Darkness softened the gaunt saguaro cactus, disguising them into tall monks, arms outspread, as though in blessing. The Harque Hala lay in serene repose as if inviting the beholder to musings of spiritual purity in the cathedral hush.

Entirely unreceptive to any invitation of the kind, Bishop sat down to remove his boots, banged sand out of them, and wished he could leave them off to ease his blistered feet. He shook sand from his clothes, brushed it from his hair, dug it out of his ears, wiped his face and neck. Meantime, he tried to find his bearings, which he had mislaid during the blinding hours. The stars told him that he faced roughly south. They didn't tell him how far off his course he might have wandered. No landmarks were visible to him. The sand spread in rippled waves, untrodden as newly fallen snow and much less convenient for walking.

His sense of direction had kept him pointed southward, more or less. He hadn't traveled in circles. But the south covered an expansive territory, and an unknowing drift here and there may well have thrown him off the course to Yellow Wells.

"Maybe I should get me a pocket compass," he muttered, spending a thought on McLean.

His voice sounded like the scrape of a rusty hinge to his own ears. He pulled his boots back on, scowling at the smart of broken blisters, and set off again in search of Don Ricardo.

He wasn't lost. Never lost. He just wasn't sure of the location of Yellow Wells in relation to his own whereabouts. Nor did his mind concede the likelihood of exhaustion, although given the lie by thirst, hunger, tiring muscles, and the aggravating effects of too much loss of sleep. He did acknowledge to himself a want of rest and sustenance, a need to replenish his vitality. He had to. Even the thought of Tandra failed to make him feel young.

The rising moon exposed Yellow Wells as a relic of

misled enterprise. It had been set up as a relay station, equipped with eating accommodations, by an ambitious stage line company that bankrupted itself trying to carry passengers where only horsemen ventured. Some optimist then turned it into a roadhouse and built large corrals, but drought struck and the trail herds shunned the dry route. Left deserted, it gave overnight shelter to occasional wayfarers. Bishop had made transient use of it a time or two in the past.

He rested on his heels, taking stock of the place, filling in from memory what he couldn't see. The broken-down stagecoach was still there, all four wheels missing. The corrals, he recalled, were stoutly built to hold half-wild cattle. They were a couple of hundred yards away from the buildings. Stamps and snuffles told that they were full of horses now.

"Here you are, Rico!" he murmured, listening to a burst of laughter that galled him.

The sandstorm had forced Don Ricardo to take shelter here, but the passing of the storm wasn't yet urging him to move on. Given a comfortable camp and a sense of security, even he could allow himself to indulge in the *mañana* habit. Or perhaps it was his *guerreros* who objected to breaking camp before morning. They were a stubborn breed, apt to balk when a lazy fit came over them.

"Here you are—and what the hell can I do about it?"

The laughter came from the main building, the only one that was still habitable, known as the lodge during the ill-fated roadhouse venture. It had housed a combined bar and restaurant in a single large room, with a small room at the end serving as the kitchen. There was a low porch out front on which the only door opened, and the windows were glassless and shuttered. Some light filtered out through cracks between sun-shrunken boards.

Bishop absently scratched the black stubble on his jaw

while he studied the lodge. The weak cracks of light had guided him to it, but now that he had got here the question of what to make of it stumped him. He was down to one gun and a few shells.

Laughter rumbled again. The *guerreros* were drinking, from the sounds, but they had more hard sense than to drink themselves stupid. They were relaxing, enjoying in retrospect the disastrous trick played on Starr and his crew of arrogant gringos, former accomplices in highly profitable, wholesale horse-stealing. That pay-off for insults far outweighed the loss of future profit.

It didn't mean they were slack. Alertness and instant action were instinctive to them.

And only that one door to the lodge.

He stood up, seeing no other recourse but to go on in there and have it out, be done with it. Devious tricks crumbled under close inspection; they became trivial antics, not worth the trying. Safe alternatives, easy expedients, cut at the roots of self-respect. The girl . . .

No. Go on in.

A part of his mind nagged him, questioning whether his decision was influenced by the thought of Tandra, or by his feud with Rico. Maybe McLean was right. Maybe he and Rico had grown inhuman in their private war, blindly inconsiderate of any other persons happening to get caught in it, to the callous extent that the fate of a young girl was secondary. Better, then, for them to shoot it out and both go down. That time had to come. The odds were on this night.

"Here goes!"

Stifling the question and its train of thought, Bishop paced slowly and soundlessly to the lodge. Nobody challenged his approach. He put his eye to a crack between boards and peered in. The section of the big room visible to him showed part of a table, an uncorked bottle of tequila, a wax candle, and numerous cigarette butts. And Don Ricardo.

Bishop touched his gun. The temptation to shoot was strong, bolstered by aches and pains. It died under a crush of reasons, some of them clearly logical, some cloudy.

Don Ricardo, arms on the table, sat gazing at the flame of the candle. His face was moody, his eyes withdrawn into private meditation. The bottle of tequila before him was full to the neck; he hadn't yet drunk from it. The candle was thick and squat, colored red: a *votivo* candle, strange possession for a man of his cynically unreligious kind. His *guerreros*, drinking and chattering, laughing, were leaving him severely alone. Don Ricardo de Risa, the Laughing One, had the *coraje*—the fit of sullen despondency that overcame all men at odd times in the drought-stricken country of leafless trees and mesquite and dusty huisache.

More than that. Watching, Bishop saw Don Ricardo lift his eyes from the candlelight. He knows, Bishop thought, I'm coming after him. He knows I'm near. He's ready for me. Damn him, he's got the instincts of a wild animal. I put my mind too much on him, and he's caught it.

Moving on, Bishop stepped onto the porch. A board groaned under his foot. The talk and laughter of the *guerreros* abruptly ceased.

"*Que es?*"

He booted the door. It scraped in an inch and held fast, barred on the inside.

"Open up, Rico, it's me!"

98

XIII

QUICK STEPS hit the floorboards. The wooden bar clattered, and Don Ricardo dragged the door open.

"*Mil diablos!*" he breathed, staring into Bishop's bloodshot eyes. The baleful look in them made him instinctively back off. "Hell will never hold you!" His own eyes registered warring crosscurrents of vexation and relief. "I felt you were coming, but I could not believe it! Where is the man I posted on watch?"

"Probably making the rounds of the corrals, or asleep." Bishop limped past him into the room. "You're too sure of yourself, Rico. It could get you in trouble. Somebody could've shot you from outside. Me, for instance."

"Thank you for bringing it to my attention."

"You're welcome."

"Are your feet sore? You limp."

"I'm sore all over."

Moving on, Bishop nodded to the don's men, ignoring the gun muzzles pointed at him. "*Buenas noches, amigos.*"

Their eyes shuttled looks from him to Don Ricardo. None of them had seen him on Calaveras Peak. He was a stranger to them by sight, and they were thrown off by the exchange of barbed amenities between him and Don Ricardo, whose attack of *coraje* had evaporated with Bishop's arrival.

"*Buenas noches,*" they rumbled in return, and sat down again to their bottles, but kept watch on him. They could sense Don Ricardo's brittle mood of expectancy. Each had his own candle, from which they lighted their brown cigarettes. And each laid a cocked gun carefully on the long table, within instant reach.

Bishop helped himself to the don's full bottle. Between

drinks he took off his boots. He sloshed stinging tequila over his feet and rubbed it in. The appearance of his bare feet, unlovely to begin with, wasn't improved by the broken blisters and sand-chafed red patches. The *guerreros* murmured comments. Don Ricardo clucked his tongue in mock sympathy.

"You should get yourself a horse, Rogue!"

"I aim to. A black one."

He tore up his bandanna, bound his feet, and eased them back into the boots. The door was shut to the small room that had been the kitchen. He handed the bottle to Don Ricardo, and motioned at the closed door.

"She in there?" he asked, and Don Ricardo, drinking, nodded. "I've come for her, Rico."

The don brought the bottle down from his mouth. He grinned quizzically. "Oh?"

"You made a deal with me."

"I did? Ah, yes. Let me see, what was it?"

"You damn-well know what it was! If I caught up with you this side of Mexico, as I've done—"

"There was one other condition, as I recall," Don Ricardo interrupted, with a slight bow of apology. "You spoke of a fantastic cache of silver. Has it changed into something else? A goldmine, perhaps, or a bag of jewels?" He spoke in an irritating drawl that he knew grated on Bishop.

"No, it's still the same silver," Bishop said, and ran his eyes over the armed men ranged along the table. "A fortune in *contrabando* silver, hidden back there on that peak, hombres! Ransom for the girl! He didn't let you know about it, did he?"

"I seldom repeat fairy tales," the don countered, and they grinned back at him, shaking their heads. "The silver stays hidden? You brought none with you?"

"Some, not much." Bishop dug his hand into a pocket of his coat. The movement caused some of the men to finger their guns. He jingled coins in his pocket. "I had to make it here on foot, thanks to a lousy thief who stole my horse!"

Don Ricardo accepted the insult with surface equanimity. "Silver is in general circulation," he pointed out. "It is easy to pick up a few pesos. They will not buy a shred of belief in your fairy tale, Rogue! You are not dealing with children!"

"These pesos are all dated twenty years back," Bishop said, "and they're tarnished. Yet the edges are sharp as if fresh from the mint. Here, I'll show you."

"Don't trouble yourself."

"You can see they were new and they've never been used in circulation. The big-time smugglers got their coins new, for full weight, as you know. This was big, so big that Russian Jack spent a lot of time and all his money on raiding it. It broke him."

"*Qué lástima!*" Don Ricardo sighed. "You bring tears to my eyes!" He wiped away an imaginary tear, and his men chuckled at the foolery. "That poor old madman! Is madness contagious? Do I perceive insanity in your obsession with this silver mirage, Rogue?"

Bishop swallowed a bilious taste of metal and salt, the taste of his concentrated anger. He had put over more than a few tricks in the past, outrageous tricks requiring monumental lies to support them, on Don Ricardo and others more-or-less of his kind. Now, telling the truth, he met rank disbelief. It was intensely aggravating.

Pulling his hand from his coat pocket, he showed it overflowing with tarnished silver pesos. He let a couple of them spill onto the table.

"Look at 'em, hombres! Thousands more where they came from! A million!"

It didn't work. Imbued with the don's flippant skepticism, the *guerreros* grinned, nodding their heads and murmuring ironically, "*Sí, sí—un millón pesos!*" Had he mentioned a sum—Bishop realized too late—of five or ten thousand, they might have given it some credence. A million pesos was incredible to them, an amount beyond count and impossible to imagine. The big gringo was loco, stricken by delusions of vast wealth.

Don Ricardo cocked an eyebrow, smiling at the handful of heavy coins. "May I take one?" he requested. They were alike, but he poised a hand over them as if languidly choosing a *dulce* from a platter held by a servant. "Just one, a souvenir—a memento of this ridiculous occasion?"

Bishop's temper exploded. His hand came up and slammed the pesos hard into the smooth, smiling face. "Take 'em all, damn you!"

The unplanned move caught Don Ricardo unprepared; it lacked forethought, finesse, everything but an uncertain value of surprise. He collided backward into the edge of the table, his astonished grunt issuing through a temporary plaster of pesos, some in his mouth. The seated men grabbed at upset bottles and rolling candles.

Having gone so far, Bishop promptly heaved the table over into the men's laps, then lunged low for the closed door of the small end-room. The candles winked out. In the scrambling uproar a gun went off. Don Ricardo cursed the shooter, who snarled back that it was an accident, that he had bullet-burned his own leg.

Blinded by the sudden darkness, Bishop rammed full into the closed door a half-stride ahead of his calculations. Its latch broke and it flew open, banging as he headed on in. The swing of it barely missed hitting Tandra. She was a white figure before him, too near to avoid, and she uttered a cry when he, trying to keep from falling over her, lifted her off her feet and bore her along for a couple of strides.

The noise of his entrance couldn't pass unheard. "Guard the door!" Don Ricardo rapped. "He's trying to steal the girl!"

Bishop's feet met something soft on the floor, and he took a header. He and Tandra sprawled together on a pallet of saddle blankets. Thinking the worst, for which he couldn't blame her, she beat at him until he made himself known to her by his voice, growling, "Quit that, I'm in enough trouble!"

He got up, listening to the men in the big room shove the table off themselves and overturn it, sorting out dropped guns and swearing their disgust at the waste of tequila. His eyes adjusted to the darkness, and he noted that the ex-kitchen was as he remembered it: no outside door, two tiny windows, shuttered. It was worse than the cave, he thought, this was a botch.

Don Ricardo crackled oaths, interspersed with bitter complaints that his *guerreros*—he was calling them everything but that—had overturned the table onto him. He had been searching under it for his sombrero, shaken off by Bishop's silver-laden clout. The mishap made Bishop feel a trifle better, and he spoke to Tandra on a note of false cheer.

"Maybe his luck's running short."

"Did Mike come with you?" she asked him.

"Mike? Oh—McLean. We started out together. Got separated."

"Then he's alive?"

"Was, last I saw him."

He shook his head at the vagaries of females. This girl had lived out of touch with civilization practically all her life, knowing no one but her half-mad grandfather. She was primitive, without a scrap of experience, of any ordinary means of making worldly comparisons, and as innocent as an infant. But she had full-grown feminine emotions. The same sense of values, the same unerring instinct for picking the wrong man.

She touched his arm in the dark. "Thank you for coming after me. I'll thank you for the rest of my life."

She was taking it for granted that he would get her safely out of this place. "I'll owe my life to you."

Several years dropped from him. "If McLean's gone under, what will you do?" he asked.

"I—" She paused. "I'll do whatever you say. I don't know the world, only Bronco City."

"You can't go back there."

"I'll go wherever you say."

He nodded. She had the makings of rare good sense, an admirable ability to adapt herself to circumstances. No hysterics. Pliable. An unspoiled girl, gifted with an intuitive perception of masculine values, she only needed the benefits of an experienced man's teachings, his guidance toward advanced enlightment. Men lived large lives, some larger than other. The feminine realm was restricted, and Tandra's had been more restricted than most.

Bishop refrained from wishing McLean harm, if McLean hadn't already met it. He did incline to the opinion that fate, if it had to deal a mortal blow, would be showing a co-operative spirit by selecting that young treasure hunter.

One of the men in the big room struck a match. Bishop cut a shot at it through the open door, and the man swore and dropped it. Immediately, gun-hammers snicked to full cock. Bishop jumped aside to cover, pulling Tandra with him. It came to him that fate—or fatality—had an eye lined in his direction. Tandra's faith in his powers was uplifting, but cold logic presented stark facts. The wall between the two rooms was flimsy, built of single boards butted together, now dried and shrunken. A bullet could penetrate the wall anywhere, flick through as if it were paper.

"Don't shoot!" Don Ricardo commanded quickly. "Don't shoot into that room! The girl!"

He would not risk killing the girl. He had not changed that much from the old days, had not coarsened to in-

104

discriminate bloodshed like a brutish *bandido*, like a depraved *americano* badman. Not yet. Bishop held Tandra to him by his left arm, feeling the trembling of her body, knowing by it that her trust in him was not limitless. She knew the score: she was his shelter, all that saved him from a hail of bullets. So she pressed closer to him, her guardian, guarding him.

As, he thought wryly, she had guarded her grandfather, Russian Jack, with her old muzzle-loader. A rare and very special girl, soft as velvet, hard as springsteel.

Freeing her from him, Bishop called, "Rico!"

Don Ricardo shushed his noisy men. "Yes?"

"It's a stand-off. You know it. Tandra's here with me. You can't show a light—I'll pick you off. You can't come in here—same reason."

"And you can't get out!"

"Right! Want to talk a deal? She—"

"No, damn you and your treacherous tricks!" rasped Don Ricardo, all injured virtue now that the trick ran against him. "Come out of there and meet me man to man!" His slammed face must have pained him.

"You and your *paisanos?*" Bishop held his gun aimed at the door. "I don't downgrade 'em, nor you. I'd take you on in a straight shoot-out, but you've got too much help! Come in here alone, Rico."

"You have an advantage, Rogue," the don said acidly. "You are in the dark. Come out!" In his wrathy indignation he was overlooking the fact that he shared the darkness.

Bishop kicked the door shut, ending the argument, and felt along the wall to one of the little windows. Its shutter creaked to his pressure; it hadn't been opened for years. Beside him, Tandra said hushedly, "It's much too small."

"Not for you. I can squeeze you through." He exerted more pressure with his hands, feet and legs braced. The shutter gave way on rusted hinges, letting a small square of moonlight into the room. "Come on!" He reached for her.

"No!" She backed away from him, shaking her head. "No!"

Angered, he whispered, "Dammit, girl, don't go mule on me now! I know Rico! He'll talk his *guerreros* into making a charge at me. They won't want it—no profit in it for 'em. But he's Rico, so they'll do it. Come on, hurry!"

"And leave you?"

"You promised to do whatever I say! To go wherever I told you!" A promise carried no weight, though, he supposed, with a girl of her uncivilized upbringing. He prepared to catch her up and force her out through the small window-opening, willing or not.

Sensing his intention, she eluded him. "I'll not run away and leave you here!" She was determinedly rebellious, and as angry as he. "You strange, strange man! What has your life been, for you to expect me to do that? What is the world like? Are people false to their friends? If so, the world must be an ugly place, and I don't want to live in it!"

Bishop blinked at her. "No," he said, "the world's okay. People are people, good and bad. I'm one of 'em."

"You're my friend. Would you leave me here?"

"No."

"And I'll not leave *you*."

He wondered how, on that desolate peak, she had learned the nature of loyalty. Perhaps loyalty was inherited, not learned. Some lost it, some didn't. That unquestioning, sacrificial loyalty of a friend who'd stick with you through hell, sink or swim. It might not do any good; it could be an encumbrance and an added liability; but in the pinch sometimes even a loner liked to know he had earned it and that he had it with him.

"All right," Bishop told Tandra. "Come to think of it,

I don't know where you could run to. We'll stick together."
He held out a hand and she took it unhesitatingly in
both of hers. "Okay?" His purpose, freighted on casual
speech, was to steady her nerves.

She echoed his last word, a strange one to her: "Okay!"

XIV

THE DOOR shuddered under a heavy blow from the butt
of a carbine. Bishop fired as it burst open. The man
who dealt the blow stood surprised for an instant; he
must have assumed that the door was fastened and
would have to be battered down. Bishop's bullet caught
him poised to deliver a second stroke. He fell against
the doorframe. Men behind him, holding guns and car-
bines, split to both sides.

Bishop thought he had hit Don Ricardo, until the man,
supported partly by the doorframe, slid farther into the
moonlight shining through the opened window. Laboriously handling his carbine, changing ends to shoot, the
wounded man spoke breathily.

"A window is open, Don Ricardo! Your girl is gone!"

"No, she's still here, Rico!" Bishop said quickly. "She
wouldn't go! Get your man out!"

"Don't shoot, Paco!" Don Ricardo rapped. "Come back
in here!"

"*Maldito—!*" grated Paco. He took a wavering step
forward, his dimming eyes searching the small room, the
carbine rising level.

In the main room a gun roared a single shot. Paco
dropped face-forward. The carbine discharged under
him.

After a silent moment a voice complained somberly,
"Don Ricardo, you shot him! You killed Paco! He was
a good man."

107

"He was the best one of you," the don said.

"Then why—?"

"It was my order that nobody shoot into that room. Not while the girl is there, in the dark."

"Paco was wounded. He forgot your order, in his pain, in his wish for vengeance."

"Yes, but he might have shot her, in his madness," Don Ricardo countered sharply.

"It troubles me," grumbled another *guerrero*. "For this *gringa* girl you kill one of us! If she is still in there, I say get her yourself!"

There were mutters of agreement. A third voice spoke up. "Let the big *gringo* have her! I take him to be a man!"

"What!" exclaimed Don Ricardo. "Would you give him his way? Let me down? After that—that low, brutish trick?"

"*Perdón.* To slap one with a pound of pesos, is that brutish? Clownish, yes. It had touches of humor."

"He tipped the table over onto you!"

"*Bien,* it was time for us to be moving on."

"He wounded Paco badly!" the don persisted, trying his best to stir them up. "Did it have humor, to see poor Paco stumble on through that door?"

"He did not shoot poor Paco in the back!" they chorused at him accusingly.

Hearing them, Bishop concluded that Rico was whistling up a stump. Men of their raw temperament couldn't be budged when the perverse mood was on them. Get on their wrong side, and nothing you did or said was right; while it lasted they'd condemn the deeds of an archangel and twist the words of a saint. In the process, conversely, they might find excuses for the devil.

Crouched low, Bishop took the opportunity to strip Paco of his gun, carbine, and shell-studded bandoleer. He slid the gun into his empty left-hand holster. The carbine was a single-shot, heavy caliber, its barrel cut down too short for accurate marksmanship at more than thirty or forty yards on a man-sized target, if that: a firearm for close range in the chaparral thickets.

He heard Don Ricardo say in a stern tone, "Enough of this nonsense! Into that room! Follow me!"

The command brought no sound of movement from the men. They refused to justify the killing of Paco, their *compadre,* by the self-claimed *aristo* who was their leader. There existed always that dangerous balance between subservience and ancient hatred, and in their lawlessness the *guerreros* had tasted independence.

"Must I go in alone, then?"

Bishop fitted a cartridge into the breech of the carbine. Rico would have to wait it out, cool off, until the pendulum of his men's prevailing mood swung to the opposite extreme. If he could afford to wait that long.

"Try it, Rico! Come on in!"

He moved over to Tandra, taking the loaded carbine to her, remembering that she could handle a heavy firearm and wasn't backward about shooting. It only mildly surprised him to find she had seated herself on the pallet of saddle blankets, seemingly in comfort. She had shown the same adjustment to peril, back in the cave. Then he saw that something was wrong, and he bent over her.

"What is it?"

She raised her face to his. "The man you shot—he saw me. My white dress in the dark. Perhaps he thought it was you. Or he was too hurt to think. He was trying to shoot me. Then de Risa killed him, and he fell, and when his gun went off . . . My ankle," she said. "I'm sorry."

"Take this carbine and cover the door. Easy on the trigger, it's cocked to go."

Bishop knelt and examined her ankle in the dim light. The carbine bullet had nicked it on the inside, chipping the bone. She had been holding the painful wound pressed with her fingers to stem the blood, and the blood was stickily clotted around it. Bishop sighed. She would not have the use of that foot for some time.

She heard his sigh, and said again, "I'm sorry."

"Be glad it's not worse." He frowned at her. "Are you apologizing for getting shot?"

"I'm giving you so much trouble."

"There's always trouble when Rico and I meet. Like mixing saltpeter and sulphur. Makes gunpowder. You happen to be the spark this time." And that, he thought after saying it, was the rock-bottom truth. Anything could set him and Rico into explosive conflict. But it wasn't much of a compliment to her, so he added, "You're worth the trouble."

A light appeared in the big room. "Rogue!" Don Ricardo rapped. "I am coming in with a candle and a gun! Alone!" It wasn't a warning. It was a challenge. He would save face and his high self-esteem at whatever cost. "I will put the candle down between us, and we'll—"

"Bring me something to use for a bandage," Bishop broke in on the terms of the proposed duel. "I just found out Tandra's shot in the ankle. Paco's bullet."

"Paco's bullet!" Don Ricardo gave a derisive snort. "And you just found out! Why didn't she tell you before now?"

"I guess she's not the complaining kind."

"This is another trick, no?"

"No, dammit, come in and see! Keep your men out."

Slowly, holding the lighted candle aloft, Don Ricardo stepped to the doorway of the small room. His alert eyes fastened on the carbine, held cocked and leveled at him by Tandra. He froze, disconcerted, until Tandra lowered the carbine as an unspoken permission for him to advance. His face, bruised and discolored, expressed a cynical belief that Bishop had lied to him, and he entered with the tautness of a tomcat exploring a kennel.

Then, seeing Tandra's blood-clotted ankle, he sucked a breath and flared out at Bishop, "I blame you for this, damn you and your meddling! She is crippled!" The wound at first sight looked worse than it actually was. "*Ay, ay, qué lástima!* So young, so spirited and graceful —and now this!"

"You are not talking about a horse," Bishop said. "She'll be okay in a few days."

The don usually had a clean white handkerchief somewhere on him, and he produced one. He bound the ankle lightly, clucking his tongue and murmuring Spanish phrases which Tandra couldn't understand, fortunately; his endearments were as unreserved as his curses, and Bishop didn't translate them for her.

In the other room the men had lighted more candles. They were talking among themselves, arguing. Their low tones hinted at conspiracy. A pounding on the door of the lodge silenced them.

A hoarse voice outside called urgently, "Bishop! If you're in there—if Tandra's with you—get her out, quick!" The pounding shook the door again. "Hurry! It's the Starr bunch! They're coming up behind me!"

Don Ricardo jumped to his feet. "Who is that?"

Bishop lifted Tandra up off the pallet. "It's McLean," he said. "I'd have bet he perished." It occurred to him that a man's ill-wishes frequently backfired on him. "Unless he's off his head, our chickens are coming home to roost, Rico."

They unbarred the door. McLean lurched in, gray from exhaustion, saying in his croaking voice, "They got on my trail after the storm." He peered unseeingly about him, the lighted candles dazzling his swollen eyes. Bishop, carrying Tandra, came into his focus and he started forward. "What've you done to her?"

"She had an accident," Bishop told him. His sore feet, bearing the added weight of the girl, roughened his

111

disposition and he demanded harshly, "Did you lead that mob here with your blasted compass?"

"No! I lost them. But they know this place. After I backtracked, I found they'd done the same, so I circled around and got here ahead of them. Tandra—!"

Bishop fended McLean off. "She can't walk, and you're not in any shape to carry her."

"Are you?" Don Ricardo inquired. "Allow me!"

"To hell with you! Let's get to the horses!"

The *guerreros* had the same idea, one which they had discussed among themselves in their discontent. They stamped to the door. A shot cracked. The first man out fell across the porch. The rest halted, looking down at him. A volley of gunfire whipped splinters from the doorframe and tore holes through the dry boards of the wall. A man turned as if to speak, and collapsed.

"They were behind me when I came by the corrals," said McLean. He still had his rifle, and he cleaned sand from the breech hurriedly. "They're sorefooted, and they act like crazy men. We don't need those candles."

"*Mil diablos!*" Don Ricardo fanned the candles out with a sweep of his sombrero. "You mean they have cut us off from the horses?"

"That's what I mean." McLean's voice came flat and quiet in the darkness. "And this place is like a paper sack. And they're out for blood. Murder. Worse. And Tandra's here." Then he burst out, "Goddam you, that's what I mean!"

The *guerreros* spilled through the door and bounded over the porch. On the run, they spun around to fire back at the dark mass of men hobbling slowly up from the direction of the corrals. One of them yelled, "Don Ricardo, I spit on you! For the *gringa* you lose us everything!" The advancing men stopped to send long shots after them.

McLean poked Bishop. "Let's go before they—"

"Her white dress," Bishop said. "Get a couple of those saddle blankets."

Don Ricardo brought the blankets. "Wait!" He darted off while Bishop and McLean spread them over Tandra. A shuttered window on the south side banged open. "Now!" he called. His pair of guns roared.

Bishop carried Tandra out. Hugging the shadowed front wall, he trod the length of the porch and dropped off the end, wincing at the shock to his feet. McLean followed him to the sheltered end of the building and peered back around the corner.

"They're holding off! No—spreading out, crawling up closer, but slow." The shooting increased, concentrated on the lodge. Don Ricardo's guns abruptly quit. "I guess they got him," said McLean. "Didn't he know he'd draw all their fire on himself?"

"He knew," Bishop said shortly. He shifted Tandra's weight onto his left arm and shoulder, freeing his right hand.

"I can try to walk," she offered.

He didn't reply, and McLean said, "I can help you carry her, can't I?"

"How far?" he asked bleakly. "The nearest town's Tonopah, about twenty miles south. Twenty miles of nothing! And they've got us cut off from there."

"West?"

"Harrisburg, fifty miles. North, Wickenburg—that's Roone's headquarters. East—"

Don Ricardo suddenly slipped around the corner and joined them. "They're coming!" he warned, rapidly reloading his guns. "We must move fast!"

"Where? How? I was talking geography. Now I'll talk sense. The girl can't walk. McLean's legs are about given out, and so're my feet. We can't run!"

"Neither can they."

"They can saddle up horses and track us down before we've gone half a mile! We've got to hide out, and it

113

better not be far. *You* run, Rico! I can make it to that busted old stagecoach, there, without them seeing me."

"So near!" murmured the don. "And Tandra?"

"If they think we've all gone, they won't spend time searching around here. Yes, Tandra hides with me. I don't see anything better for her, do you?" Bishop turned his face to her. "Or do you?"

"Whatever you say," she said.

McLean looked at her. "It's an awful risk!"

"Any port in a storm! You suit yourself." Bishop set off to the wheelless relic, keeping the lodge between himself and Starr's advancing crew. Its leather curtains hung in remnants and it had been stripped of its running gear.

He helped Tandra into the coach and ducked in after her. The facing seats were worn and split, spilling their cotton padding; packrats had been at them. He closed the door, but it opened again. McLean and Don Ricardo hastily burrowed in.

"*Con permiso,*" the don murmured as if boarding a fully equipped Concord about to pull out.

Bishop eyed him expressionlessly. "You son!"

Don Ricardo returned a cool glance. He crossed his legs and leaned back. "My boots were not made for walking."

"Nor mine! But I had to walk here from Bronco City, damn your horse-thief hide!"

"Ss-t!" McLean hissed. "Here they come! Drop your feud will you? Tandra's here!" He was so concerned with Tandra that he didn't realize that the noise of the oncoming Starr mob drowned out smaller sounds. The footsore men were shouting, cursing, as they advanced.

A flash of light wiped the interior of the coach.

"What the hell's that?" Bishop asked, twisting around to see the cause, and answered his own question. "The lodge is on fire! Rico, did you—?"

"I did!" Don Ricardo confessed. "It will be visible for

114

miles around. I wanted to make Starr anxious to leave. It's empty country, but he knows there's always a risk anywhere of lawmen or a troop of soldiers on patrol. And the fire should scare the horses so his men can't handle them all."

"And it'll light us up, damn your figuring!"

"I didn't foresee having to take cover in this thing. As I said before—so near!"

XV

FLAMES POURED from the lodge and licked upward, creating their own air-drafts that carried smoke billowing high. Seared patches of walls blackened, burst alight like kindling wood, and ran together with tearing, popping sounds. The roof caught fire and split open, releasing a mighty column of sparks. From the corrals rose a commotion of squeals and whinnyings.

"Get to the horses before they bust the fences down!" Starr shouted. In the glare of the fire he looked less than human, with his long neck, ill-shaped body, and shock of yellow hair. A makeshift man, put together from odd pieces, but endowed with raw strength and stamina.

He had come through the ordeal in better condition than his men, for he stood on his feet and gestured forcefully at them. They rested on the ground, slackfaced, staring dully at the burning lodge as if it had robbed them of their revenge. The penned horses could be heard milling wildly about, made frantic by their instinctive dread of fire.

"The corrals, goddam it!" Starr bellowed. "Come on, you lily-toed nursemaids!"

Most of them made weary efforts to obey. Five stayed lying on the ground. One, dabbing his eye, complained,

"Ain't you driv us enough? Them fences'll hold. They was built to hold cows. I got sand in my eye. It's all swole."

"We got to have horses to ride after Risa and the others, don't we?" Starr demanded. "They're afoot." He hit his holster a slap. "I won't never rest till we get 'em!"

"Sure. Bring me a horse an' I'll ride with you. I couldn't see to rope me a saddle-maker's wooden horse in the noon sun."

Another of the reclining five said, "I can't walk one more step if it was to Christmas."

In the broken-down old coach, McLean whispered, "If they all take off . . . But I guess not."

Bishop watched Starr plod toward the corrals, his men shambling after him. "He'll leave a few behind to ride guard on the corrals. Bound to. And the fire lights up everything. But we need horses. Got any ideas, Rico?"

"None worth trying until the fire burns down. Tandra, do you have pain?"

"I'm all right."

They crouched below the sills of the side windows, their faces shadowed by the tattered leather curtains. The small space between the seats cramped them, but they dared not move. The glare of the fire brightened. They began to feel its increasing heat. The coach stood out starkly on the bare ground.

Don Ricardo peered malevolently at the five men who had not followed Starr to the corrals. "Damn them!" he breathed. "If they had gone with the others, we might have slipped out and circled wide around, Rogue. At the right time we might have got horses."

"Maybe the chance'll still come. Freeze, Rico! That feller's looking straight this way!"

"I see him! The one with sand in his eye?"

"That's the one."

The man took his good eye off the coach and said to the four around him, "I been thinkin'. You s'pose there's

116

any grub in that ol' coach, or water fit to wash my eye with?"

He drew negative responses.

"Ten to one says there ain't."

"Hundred to one!"

"Why the hell would there?"

"Well, folks've used this place for a stopover," he argued. "Like Risa. Somebody mighta cached grub an' water for the return trip, y'know. That'd be as safe a cache as any round here. I bet nobody ever looks in it." He dabbed at his inflamed eye. "Jeez, I'd sure like some clean water for this!"

"Why don't you go look?"

"Whyn't you?"

"It's your idea an' your goddam eye!"

"Huh—friends! I've had better friends in jail!"

They grunted tired laughs at him, asking which of many jails he meant. Having argued himself half-heartedly into exerting the effort, he heaved sluggishly to his feet. "I find anything, it's all mine!" he said unhopefully, and they passed jeering comments on his scavenging habits.

Walking painfully splay-footed, he approached the coach, his dejected manner that of a man expecting no luck. He stopped at the door and tried the handle, but Bishop had hold of the inside handle and blocked it tight. Thinking it was stuck, the man let go of it after a dispirited attempt. He brushed back hanging tatters of leather curtain and poked his head in.

His good eye bulged and his mouth gaped open for the instant before Don Ricardo whacked him smartly with a gun butt. He slid out, down, against the outside of the coach. The four men, idly watching him, sat up staring. One burst out laughing.

"Bumped his fool head an' knocked himself out! I be damned if that ain't the funniest—" He stopped.

The other three weren't laughing with him. "What's wrong?" he asked them.

"Didn't move fast enough to knock himself out! What'd he bump his head on in there? Somethin' bumped *him!*" The speaker, the man who had said he couldn't walk another step, drew his gun. "There's somebody in that coach! Cover it! Call Starr back!"

"If you're wrong, he'll—"

"I ain't wrong!" He loosed off two shots; they were meant as a signal, but he didn't waste them in the air.

The two bullets struck the coach with a solid sound, a sound that settled a question that had occupied Bishop for the past moment. The coach had been stoutly constructed for the hardest possible usage, like a cross-country mail wagon. It was now an old relic, but its heavy woodwork could withstand gunfire. The two bullets hadn't penetrated on through.

Don Ricardo promptly paid out a shot in return. "I made a truthful man of that one," he remarked. "Not another step! I wish we could make a break before all the others come up. Now would be the time, eh?"

He was speaking to Bishop; it was McLean who, taking the words as a hint, said, "If you want to try it, what's to stop you? You're able." McLean was working the numbness out of his arm, and didn't see the don's face grow hard and clear-cut. "We'll cover for you."

Bishop's headshake restrained Don Ricardo from delivering a bloody-minded retort. McLean went on working his arm, Tandra holding his rifle and watching him.

"But they would be hot after us, of course, and we can't travel fast or far. So"—Don Ricardo shrugged fatalistically—"that is that!"

McLean raised his head to say something. Meeting the don's eyes, he left it unsaid. The don's eyes coolly rebuked him, reduced him to secondary rank, stripped him of any notion that staying to the end was a special virtue deficient in a badman. McLean's gaunt face flushed, for by that look he knew then that he had blunderingly dared to take a condescending tone to a seasoned veteran. Not even Bishop would have done it seriously.

"*Mira!* They come! Luck, Rogue!"

"Luck, Rico!"

The three men remaining from the five, having scrambled out of close range, yelled to the mob returning from the corrals, telling them they had somebody boxed in the old Concord. Swarming wide around the burning lodge, the mob came on without halting. Their temper had changed from lethargy to furious exasperation.

"Kill-crazy!" McLean exclaimed. "They don't even stop to shoot!" He rested his rifle on the sill of a side window. "If I can pick off Starr—"

"Don't wait," Bishop said. "Don't let 'em get in close. They'll be all over us. Let 'em have it now!"

Four guns and a rifle hammered from the coach. The sudden volley broke the insane onrush. Starr's men wavered, fell back, splitting into groups. They cursed the three men, blaming them for misleading them into thinking the coach contained only one man.

Starr barged among them, gathering them around him, shouting, "It's Risa we got in there, I lay my life! Risa an' the big feller, an' that other'n!"

Don Ricardo nimbly reloaded his guns. "His life?" he murmured, and cracked off three shots at him. The hanging smoke, flickering light, and long range combined to make shooting chancy. His bullets whipped among the men around Starr. Then the men dropped flat to crawl forward, firing from the ground, and that advance had to be beaten off.

McLean ejected an empty cartridge case from his rifle and searched fruitlessly through his pockets. "I'm out of shells."

"So'll I be soon, this keeps up," Bishop said. "Quit

annoying 'em, Rico." After punching out the empties, he found that he had eight shells left. He thumbed four into each gun, set the cylinders, cocked the hammers—methodical acts requiring no thought, no conscious attention to the present, the past, the future. He glanced at Tandra, and thought intruded. Hard thought.

He had been in Indian fights. Apaches. Commanches. Yaquis below the border. Desperate fights, women and children sometimes involved. Fights when men looked in black despair at their weaker kin; men resolving between mercy-killing and torture.

Starr's men weren't savages, so-called. They weren't fighting for their land, for their ancient rights. But they were white savages, scum. They were raiders, white raiders, renegades who bore no more decent respect toward women then they did for other people's lives and property.

Don Ricardo fanned smoke away from before his eyes. "Starr is dividing them into two groups," he said. "We know what that means!" Presently he added, "Yes, they're moving to the left and right of us. A nutcracker!"

The blind ends of the coach, fore and aft, gave protection to Starr's maneuver. "When they start closing in," Bishop said, "we'll just have to lean out and—"

"And get our heads blown off! I knew this coach was a bad choice! The fire will show us up to them!"

"This coach was my idea. The fire was yours. Between us we've pulled one hell of a bobble, yeah!"

Don Ricardo put his head out and quickly withdrew it. "They're closing in on both sides," he reported gloomily. "The jaws of the nutcracker! Rogue—"

"How near are they?"

"Give them ten seconds more. Rogue, what shall we do about—her?"

"She's my problem," Bishop replied shortly, and the don's eyes searched his bleak face.

"Have you ever had to kill a woman?"

"Once. After some scabby brush-tramps got through with her. Mexican girl."

The don sighed heavily, cocking his guns. "They should be near enough by now."

"Let's get to it."

Poking out his head and one gun, Bishop fired four times, sighting his shots at the column of men closing in on the left. The men crouched, blazing back. He shoved the emptied gun into its holster and changed over to the other.

Don Ricardo, giving his attention to the advancing column on the right, uttered a hissing gasp and rocked back from the window. He dropped his guns. While making to clutch his head, he fell across McLean and Tandra. He muttered a faint word and lay limp. McLean rolled him off, having difficulty doing it in the cramped space, saying, "Where are his guns?"

Bishop didn't answer. He spent three of his last four shells and holstered the gun, and snatched up the don's at his feet. Their lean bone butts didn't fit his hands, but he found their actions easy, honed close to hair-trigger.

"Get the shells from his belts and let me have 'em, McLean!"

Bobbing in and out of the door-window between fast shots, he glimpsed the ungainly figure of Starr weaving through his men, head thrust forward on its long neck. He lined a bullet at Starr and saw him pitch to his knees. A shout went up. The gunfire dwindled. The shout was repeated by several voices, and it ceased.

The next time Bishop put his head out, all the men had halted and were staring about them, not at the coach but toward the outer limits of the firelight. He heard then in the sudden stillness a muffled and choppy clopping of many hoofs and a faint jingling of bridle bits.

The horse-sounds pressed in from all sides, the horses

121

held to a walk. A harsh voice hailed, "Throw down your guns, it's the law an' plenty of it!"

A cordon of horsemen emerged into the firelight, advancing in a steadily tightening circle. Starr got up off his knees and broke into a stumbling trot toward the corrals, and there was a surge to follow him. A volley crashed instantly from the horsemen. The merciless slaughter froze the two groups motionless.

"Throw down them guns an' put your hands up! We'd as soon kill the whole lot o' you horse-thieves, if that's how you want it!"

Don Ricardo moved, groaned, sat up on the floor of the coach holding his bloodied head. "*Que?*" he mumbled bemusedly. "*Que?*"

"It's Roone," Bishop told him. "Roone with a Wickenburg posse. The little cuss made fast time."

"My head! Smashed! I . . . What? Roone? With law?"

"Big law. You got clipped. A horse-sized headache, eh? You'll get over it in time for trial."

"*Mil diablos!* My guns—!"

"Forget 'em. They're collecting all guns."

The horsemen converged inward like a closing noose, rounding in Starr's men, forcing them into a tightly packed bunch. They were cowmen from the Wickenburg district, from the ranches of the cattlemen's association that had suffered heavy losses from horse raids. They weren't disposed to handle their prisoners with any considerateness. A squad dismounted and shouldered roughly in among them, gathering up their guns."

"Rope 'em!"

Roone hadn't troubled to pronounce a formal mass arrest or to name charges. One of Starr's men had the temerity to raise a complaint about it; he was a bunkhouse-lawyer type and he began quoting law, touching on citizen's rights and due processes. A cowman fisted him full in the mouth.

Roone's snappy voice sounded again. "Bishop! Risa!

McLean! Come out! Bring the girl if you've got her!"

McLean, helping Tandra, moved to comply with the command. Don Ricardo pushed him back.

"Wait—wait! Let us think! Rogue, isn't there something we can try? Anything!"

Bishop looked out at guns lined at the coach on all sides. He shook his head slowly, thinking of the murderous little bounty hunter's vindictiveness. The presence of the posse might have some moderating effect on Roone, at least as far as Tandra was involved. The cowmen wouldn't stand for taking vengeance on a woman.

"Not a damn thing, Rico. He's ringed us in tight. Got enough men to—"

"I've never surrendered to lawmen!"

"Be a new experience for you. For me too."

"They'll lynch me!"

"Another new experience."

The possemen shifted warily, impatiently. "Come out!" Roone repeated. "Right now, or we'll blast you out!"

XVI

Bishop vacated the coach, supporting Tandra, who hopped beside him on one foot, his arm around her. The possemen stared, unprepared for the sight of a crippled girl clad in a white robe and a couple of saddle blankets. Somewhat embarrassed, they lowered their array of ready firearms. Bishop mentally chalked up a credit to native chivalry—which he had banked on.

McLean got out next, and lastly Don Ricardo, bloody-headed, holding his sombrero in his hand. The possemen eyed the don sternly. A Mexican horse-thief. Short shrift for him. American hell-raisers manufactured more than sufficient trouble for domestic consumption. Foreign imports had to be firmly discouraged.

Roone touched his horse forward and drew up before them. His round eyes bored at them, coldly triumphant, taking in with malicious pleasure their visible hurts and injuries. "You had a showdown, huh?"

"How did you know where to find us?" McLean asked.

"I can read signs, an' I can out-think most dodgers," Roone stated. "I always win in the long run. Get your hands up along with the rest, Southerner!"

"Why? What laws have I broken?"

"You assaulted a federal officer—me! You're in with horse thieves an' outlaws! If I need any more charges to put you away, I'll think of 'em!" From his saddle Roone launched an upward kick at McLean's face. McLean jerked back, and Roone's spur missed his eye by an inch. "That goes for you too, Bishop! An' the girl. Assault with a deadly weapon! Attempted murder! Complicity in criminal acts! I've got you prize jokers where I want you!"

"Quite a haul for one night," Bishop commented, watching for a kick at his face. "The bounty ought to satisfy you."

"I done what I set out to do. A clean sweep. I'll make the most of it!" Roone heeled his horse, bringing it sidling to ram into Bishop and Tandra. With his free hand Bishop caught the bridle and forced the horse to a standstill. Roone stuck a gun at him. "Leggo my bridle!"

"Not if you aim to trample the girl's feet! She's already injured. Anybody can see that."

A protesting rumble rose from the cowmen who heard Bishop's words, which he spoke loudly for them to hear. One of them called out, "Draw the line, Roone! We ain't here to chouse women!"

Roone sucked in his thin lips. Intolerant of anyone's interference, he glared around at the speaker. His bulldog chin protruded like a blunt chisel. "She's a hellcat! She shot me!"

"She's a girl. She's hurt. Lay off!" The speaker was middle-aged. He wore a plain ring on the third finger of his left hand. A family man. A ranch owner or range boss. "Take it out on the Mexican, if your gall burns. That we'll stand for. Not the girl. Leave her be."

Frustrated, knowing no difference, in his barrenly cold-killing life, between men and women, recognizing only the solid fact of the weight of opinion, Roone pointed his gun at Don Ricardo. "Give up your guns!" Then, seeing that the don's holsters were empty, he grated at Bishop, "Yours! Quick!"

Bishop drew his guns and dropped them on the ground. He looked down at them, one empty, one containing a single shell, and said in a low voice, "You got us, but you miss the big thing. The thing that took me to Bronco City. The silver. Big! Bigger than your blood money. Bigger by far!"

Roone, round eyes glinting, feigned casual scorn. "I've heard you talk about silver. So?"

"It's there," Bishop said. "A ton of it. *Contrabando* silver. Mexican pesos." He scraped a few tarnished coins from his coat pocket and displayed them. "Like these. Look at 'em. They came fresh from the mint twenty years ago. I showed some to Rico, here, but he's a disbelieving fool. You're not. You know how the *contrabando* raiders operated. You knew, years ago, about Russian Jack, Sandy Mac, all the others."

Roone nodded, inspecting the coins. "Sure. I knew about 'em." He ran the tip of his tongue over his lips, and demanded, "Do I get the letter you an' McLean spoke about, or do I search you for it?"

"Here." Bishop took the letter from his pocket and gave it to him. "Read it for yourself. Maybe you can figure out from it where the silver's cached. I doubt it."

Roone snatched the letter. He went through the written pages slowly, his lips shaping each word, brows furrowed.

"All right. Sandy Mac says here they cached the silver under Clear Day. It took 'em half the night or more. Must've been a lot o' silver. Clear Day. Who knows where that is?"

"I do. I'm the only one who knows." Bishop fished part of a broken cigar from his breast pocket, eyed it disparagingly, clamped it between his teeth. "Got a match?"

Roone started a hand automatically toward his pockets, and stopped it. Entirely humorless, he grated, "You'll hang in Wickenburg! As chief witness for the prosecution, I can swear your life away! You an' McLean, an' the Mexican. I'll see to it the girl don't get off free, neither. The court an' jury will believe anything I say."

"If there's a trial. If you take us in alive."

"If!"

"*Ley del fuego!*" murmured Don Ricardo, and Bishop nodded his understanding of the grim term. Shot while attempting escape. *Ley del fuego.* The excuse of bounty-hunting killers like Roone, accepted without question. Condoned because it saved the expense and time-consuming bother of a public trial. Lynch law's close cousin, wearing a cloak of legality.

Roone said insinuatingly, holding his voice down, "The silver won't do you any good when you're dead! Where is it?"

"Are you offering a deal?" Bishop asked him. He found a match and lit his broken cigar, trimming it to burn evenly. "It'll have to be good. The silver's worth a fortune."

"Your life for it!"

"What else d'you offer?"

"The girl, if you want her." Roone shuttled an opaque, sexless glance at Tandra. Grudgingly he added, "An' McLean."

"Horses?"

"Take your pick. Where's the silver?"

"I'll tell you that," Bishop said, "when we're in saddle and set to go. Not before. I don't trust you."

"You are right, Rogue!" Don Ricardo put in. "We must have good horses under us before we—"

"Did I include you in the deal?" Bishop asked him. "I don't recall that I did."

"You overlooked me in the, er, stress of the moment," Don Ricardo responded forgivingly. "Now, the terms of the deal. I suggest that I ride ahead with Tandra, while you—" He caught Bishop's eye fastened icily on him, and desisted. "Perdón!"

"Don't talk till you're talked to, Rico!" Bishop told him in Spanish. "We're dead ducks if I bobble this deal!" To Roone he said, "The four of us. We get horses. You allow us time for our getaway. Well?"

"My horse is—" Don Ricardo began.

"Shut your mouth!" Roone rapped at him. "You don't count in this!" To Bishop he said more moderately, "All right, that's the deal. You get your horses. You tell me where the silver's hid. Then you can go."

He lowered a look at the letter, still in his hand, doing it to hide his eyes, but not before Bishop glimpsed his relentless animosity, his hatred.

"Watch him!" Don Ricardo breathed to Bishop. "His word is nothing!"

"I know it!" Bishop whispered back from the side of his mouth. "Be ready!"

They both eyed Roone faithlessly. The deadly little bounty hunter had no intention of turning them loose. He was out for all he could get, including revenge for slights, insults, and hurtful manhandling. His writhing ego demanded revenge, placing it for once above hard cash. In his warped view, treachery became cleverness. He had no code. To kill, cleverly and coldly, was the apex of his craft. Cash-bounty Roone.

"First, McLean and the girl get horses and they ride

127

on ahead," Bishop said. He thought for a moment. "Then we—Rico and me—we take off. Agreed?"

Roone, his eyes still lowered, nodded. "After you tell me where's the silver hid, you go free." He jiggled his cocked gun. "Not before!"

"Okay. Give McLean and the girl their horses."

"Why them?"

"They're both damaged. Her foot. His arm."

"Oh. All right, them first. A minute first. Then you an' Risa." Roone's eyes flickered upward, whitely, for an instant revealing his malevolent spite. Then, curving his thin lips in a smile that was altogether unnatural to him, he called to the possemen who were closest, "Give 'em their horses an' saddles!"

Cries of protest went up from the possemen.

"What—*them?*"

"The gal, yeah—but not them!"

"Hang 'em!"

Still smiling his false smile, Roone announced loudly, "I'm in charge here! I'm a federal officer—a United States special marshall I order you to give these people their horses an' saddles, on penalty of flagrant disobedience of a federal officer! I swore you in, ev'ry man-jack o' you!" He smiled around at them, adding, "I know what I'm doing—I always know! Give 'em their horses an' saddles. McLean an' the girl first, then these two."

"Your posse stays back when we take off," Bishop said to him. "We don't want to tempt anybody to shoot before we get out of range."

"Sure. Only me goes with you beyant the corrals. That's when you'll tell me where the silver's cached. They don't have to know about it. Only me, nobody else. Good enough?"

Bishop nodded. "It'll do," he said. But he didn't believe it, not for an instant, knowing Roone's insatiable lust for revenge.

McLean and Tandra, mounted on stolen horses and Mexican saddles that had belonged to Don Ricardo's men, looked at Bishop uncertainly, not able to credit the reality that they were free to leave together.

"What're you waiting for?" he demanded.

"For you," Tandra answered him.

"Well, don't! The deal is, you get a head start. Be on your way!"

"And leave you? It's not right!"

"We'll catch up with you," Bishop said. He stood holding the bridle of his black, sharply aware of Roone's gun trained on him. "Got a piece of business with Roone first."

"Get moving before I change my mind!" Roone threatened, and McLean and Tandra started their horses off. He motioned at the cowmen who had cut the horses out of the corral, sending them back to the waiting posse. "Okay, Bishop, now for the silver!"

"Don't I get my guns?"

"Not likely! I want the answer to that Clear Day riddle, right now!"

"And after I give it to you, then what?"

"Then you an' Risa can go. Come on, no tricks!"

"You're holding your gun on me," Bishop said. "I don't take it for a sign of good faith." He gazed past Roone at the posse. The lodge was burning low. The cowmen couldn't see as far as to the corrals. They sat motionless, their attitudes listening, expectant. "You could kill me in a wink, no objections from your Wickenburg lynch-party!"

"I aim to do that, if you don't come through!" snapped Roone, but he lowered his gun. "You're making time for McLean an' the girl's getaway, ain't you?"

"You're smart," Bishop complimented him. "It's queer you can't figure out the Clear Day thing for yourself. Maybe not so queer, though. You don't drink."

129

Roone blinked. "What's that got to do with it?"

"At your age, a drinking man would know. By never touching whiskey, you left a hole in your education." Bishop glanced at Don Ricardo. "Rico, you're a drinker. What labels d'you remember?"

The don, standing tensely by his palomino, shook his head. "I've never cared much for American whiskey. It is, as your great George Washington once observed, stinking stuff. Tequila, good aguardiente, first-rate wines —yes. But whiskey—"

"You're as ignorant as Roone," Bishop told him. "There've been some fine brands of whiskey. Used to be better stuff, according to the old-timers. Especially old prospectors and miners. I've listened to 'em in barrooms, arguing the merits of whiskey brands you never hear of nowadays. Haven't you?"

"Oh, er, of course," Don Ricardo assented, as totally bewildered as Roone, but doing his best to play along. "Let me think. Golden Sunshine—yes, they speak of that. And wasn't there something called Parker's Old Special?"

"Right," Bishop agreed. "Every mining camp had its favorite brand. Still do. The one they blow most about was called Clear Day. It came in square bottles, like nearly all those—"

"What're you gettin' at?" Roone burst out. "It's the silver I want to hear about, not booze!"

"—like nearly all those empties down the gully slope behind the Morning Glory," Bishop finished his sentence. "The labels are weathered off, but they're Clear Day bottles. Bronco City liked that brand."

"You're guessin'!"

'Am I? It's in Sandy Mac's letter that he and his pals buried their loot under Clear Day. That back room didn't cave in and fall of its own accord. They chopped the props out from under it. They let the roomful of empties smash down the slope and cover what they wanted covered. It's the one place Russian Jack never thought to search."

Roone breathed raggedly, wanting to believe, yet skeptical. "It don't sound just right," he muttered. "Somethin' tells me you're lyin'!" He stared keenly at Don Ricardo. "You don't believe it neither!"

"I believe every word!" vowed the don, swiftly masking his expression of awed incredulity. "It is entirely logical and has the ring of truth!"

"I gave you a few of those silver pesos," Bishop reminded Roone. "Where d'you think I found 'em? Look 'em over again." He felt his pocket. "I've got a couple more here."

Roone took out the pesos, frowning, and dropped his stare to them. "They don't prove much o' what you say."

Bishop drew his hand from his pocket, holding one of Don Ricardo's bone-handled guns, which he had kept in reserve. He said in a deep rasp, "Drop your gun and back up! Quick, drop it, you kill-hungry little bastard!"

Roone jerked, hesitated a second, and let his gun fall to the ground. He stepped back from it. Small, incoherent grunts came from his throat. His round eyes glared almost maniacally at Bishop, as though the gunfighter had committed an atrocious and unbearable crime against him.

In the dying light of the burned-out lodge the crowd of possemen began moving impatiently, all faces turned toward the corrals. Resenting Roone's high-handed action, the waiting made them restless. One of them hailed, "Don't take all night, Roone! What goes on there?"

"Sing out that everything's okay!" Bishop said.

Roone looked at the gun covering him, then at the saturnine face above it, calculatingly. Faithless, himself, to any code, he recognized without respect the principles that hampered some men from practicing safe homicide. He could risk gambling that Bishop might still draw the line at shooting a disarmed man.

Reading his mind, Bishop took a long swipe at him with the gunbarrel. Roone dodged back from it, and squalled, "Bishop's got the drop on me!"

XVII

DON RICARDO vaulted into his saddle and put spurs to the palomino before he toed into the tapadero stirrups. Bishop followed him on the black, not blaming him for taking off so fast. Half the possemen were hitting their horses forward, leaving the rest to guard the prisoners.

Gunfire spattered. It was reckless shooting, Roone being in the line of fire. Roone shouted, "I'll get you, Bishop! I'll get you!" Retrieving his dropped gun, he ran out from the corral fence. Bishop slung back a shot that drove him to cover.

"I'll get you! I'll track you down!" Roone was screaming it. "If it takes the rest o' my life . . ."

The palomino shied, went mad. It swerved across the black's path, head low and back humped high, crowhopping. Don Ricardo turned a desperate face to Bishop. "My horse is hit!" He kicked loose of the stirrups.

Bishop reached out his arm, an automatic act independent of past scores and grudges. Blindly erratic, the dying palomino collided into the black, broadside. The impact jarred it off its feet. Don Ricardo caught Bishop's outstretched arm as the animal took its floundering spill, and scrambled up behind him.

"Damn the luck!" He drummed his boots against the flanks of the racing black. "A chance bullet!"

"Chance? That palomino showed up in the dark like Tandra's dress," Bishop said. "Quit booting my horse!"

"*My* horse!"

"Mine now. If this gait's too slow for you, get off and run! Be easier on the horse."

"Riders ahead!" the don warned. He felt around Bishop's middle for a gun. "Two!"

"McLean and Tandra." Bishop knuckled the stealthily exploring hand. "Damned if they didn't turn back for us. Keep your fingers where they belong."

"You've got my guns!"

"Mine now. All right, McLean, Tandra, it's us."

"We heard the shooting, McLean said, reining in, "and we came back to—"

"You'll hear more," Bishop interrupted him. "Roone wasn't letting you go. He aimed to run you down, after he shot us. He's coming with about twenty of his Wickenburg toughs. He'll be after us from here on, anywhere we go, if we can't shake him off. And no trial if we're caught!"

"Hurry, Rogue!" urged Don Ricardo. "We have hard riding to do."

"And my horse carrying double!"

"Misfortunes never come singly. Without a gun I feel stark naked."

"Where do we go?" Tandra asked.

"South." Bishop touched the black onward. "We've got to beat 'em to Tonopah, with time to spare for getting outfitted there. Fresh horses, guns and shells, grub—everything we need for a long dodge." McLean and Tandra fell in behind, but he called to them, "No, you ride ahead and set the pace. Set it fast! I won't be far back, unless this horse gets tired of carrying us both."

Riding on past with Tandra, McLean said, "You could unload your passenger!"

"I'm bearing it in mind," Bishop responded.

"He's done worse!"

"Matter of opinion."

They raced southward, aware of a heavy pounding in their rear. "Rogue," said Don Ricardo, "it was a mistake to make Roone believe in that mythical silver! You

133

were too convincing. But you didn't convince him it's hidden under those broken bottles!"

"I couldn't prove it," Bishop allowed. "If I had, it wouldn't have changed him about killing us."

"True. But you have him believing that you hold the secret to a ton of silver! God help you if he ever gets you cornered again! That little manhunter hates you like Satan hates the saints, excuse the expression. A ton of silver! What wouldn't he do for it? A slow fire and a skinning knife—"

"Most likely he thinks you share the secret. Didn't I mention to him I'd told you about it?"

"*Mil diablos*, yes!"

"And there's considerable bounty on your head that he's out to collect. He hates McLean too, and Tandra for scoring his arm. I don't foresee him quitting our trail in the near future."

Don Ricardo attempted to ease his uncomfortable seat behind Bishop. "Mexico? By way of Agua Caliente?"

Bishop nodded, keeping sight of McLean and Tandra. "The horse-thief route. A hungry route, as you well know. But it's that, if we can pick up what we need in Tonopah."

"The sky is breaking light in the east. This has been a night of disasters for me. Perhaps today will be better."

"Perhaps. Don't lean on it. I might have to drop you off."

Don Ricardo fastened a tighter grip on Bishop's coat. He craned his head around for a backward look. "I can't see Roone's posse. Could it be we have outrun them?"

"It's more likely they've cut off on another route to Tonopah. They know that's where we're heading for. Let's hope we don't find 'em waiting for us there."

"A dark thought! It makes me wish we didn't have to go there."

"What else can we do?" Bishop asked. "Hit for Mexico on tired horses? Take to the hills and hide out? Once

134

they got onto our tracks they'd soon run us down. We couldn't put up much of a fight. Roone—"

"I know," Don Ricardo sighed, "I know. Roone could get us posted on the military telegraph if necessary, and have the country swarming with manhunters. A dastardly invention, that clicking machine! Tonopah it is."

"It better be, or we're cooked!"

"My head is splitting."

"Wear your hat over your other ear."

The keeper of the general store, the only store of consequence in the town, perceiving that his two customers were in a pressing hurry, called a youth from the rear to help serve them. If their hard-used appearance stirred his interest, he veiled it behind blank eyes and an impassive manner. His stock of merchandise covered everything that anyone could require within reason. Strangers in haste didn't haggle over prices; nor did they welcome inquisitiveness.

Bishop selected a pair of forty-fours, bought shells for them and for McLean's rifle, and paid the bill from his money belt. While loading them, he called to McLean, "How about it?"

McLean finished filling two grub-sacks and tied their necks together. He slung them over his shoulder. "I'm through."

"Okay, let's see what Rico's done about horses."

"No livery stable in this town," the storekeeper said. "It's a small town. Folks only come in for—"

"We noticed."

They left the general store, as briskly as bank robbers. Tandra was holding the three lathered horses and keeping watch up the empty street. The only other horse visible was a roan mare standing at a barroom hitchrack, flicking flies.

Don Ricardo came out of the barroom, saying as he

crossed over, "I've found a man who has horses to sell or trade, on his ranch a few miles out. Here he is."

A burly man followed him from the barroom. "At the right price," he said, and looked at them. "The right price," he repeated, making his meaning clear. They were plainly on the run. He could drive a hard bargain.

"That your mare?" Bishop queried.

"She is. She's fair sample of what I've got on my place. Fast horses. You got money? I mean real money."

"Some. Let's go to your place and talk trade."

The rancher shook his head. "Cash." Deliberately taking his time, he rolled a cigarette, while giving Tandra an all-over inspection. "Your horses have been hard rid."

"They're still worth trading," McLean said.

"Not to me." Searching through his pockets for a match took the rancher another minute. He found one, broke its head off in the striking, and began the lengthy process of searching for another.

Bishop handed Don Ricardo his pair of bone-handled guns. The don accepted them thankfully. McLean, his nerves stretched, exclaimed, "Dammit, man, talk business!"

"My price is five hundred a head, cash in advance."

"Five hundred, sight unseen? You're crazy!"

"Too high for you? Guess it'll have to be a trade then."

"That's better. Our horses—"

"No." The rancher's gaze roved back to Tandra. "I'd trade for the filly." He failed to see McLean ball his fists. "I need a housekeeper on my place. I'm sick o' my own cookin'."

"She would not do you," Don Ricardo told him. "She has never kept house. We'll go and look at your horses now."

"She looks a likely one to learn what I'd teach her," said the rancher. "What's your rush? I got all day." He backed off, his slab face paling, as McLean and the don stepped toward him. "Take it easy, I was just jokin'!"

Tandra, watching northward, called swiftly, "Here they come!"

A dozen riders appeared at the north end of the straggling street, converging in from both sides. The sight of them didn't deter McLean from taking a punch at the rancher, mashing his cigarette over his mouth. Don Ricardo clubbed the man in passing and sprinted on to the roan mare.

Bishop slapped Tandra's mount and sprang into his saddle. "Lean low!" he said, expecting gunfire. None came. The dozen riders cantered heavily into the street like a squad of badly drilled cavalrymen. They didn't hasten gait, didn't raise a weapon. A few townspeople came out to look at them curiously and call questions. The riders, not replying, kept their attention severely forward on the fleeing four.

McLean, catching up with Bishop and Tandra, called, "How come they're not shooting at us? Afraid of hitting Tandra? That wouldn't trouble Roone! He's there in front."

Bishop shrugged one shoulder. There were other problems to worry about. A hundred miles to the Mexican line, on tired horses unless they could pick up fresh mounts somewhere along the route. Hungry country, water scarce. No rest; Roone would see to that. No sleep, and they were hollow-eyed for want of it.

Don Ricardo flashed up on the roan mare. He asked the same question: "Why don't they shoot?" Then wary suspicion rushed into his dark eyes, and he raced on forward. No doubt about it, the rancher had spoken the truth when he said the mare was fast. It could run like a racehorse.

It could also swap ends in full stride like a cowpony cutting out a nimble yearling. Don Ricardo spun it around and came tearing back. " 'Buscado!" he spat. "Turn off!"

Horsemen charged into the south end of the street.

Those advancing from the north end hit up their mounts. Roone, for once using an oath, rapped, "Damn that Mexican! Shoot! Shoot!"

Bishop, with Tandra and McLean close behind, swerved over and took to the nearest gap between buildings, no choice in the matter. Don Ricardo passed them and held the lead, the roan mare setting a stiff pace for their horses. They came out onto catclaw land that stretched barrenly westward to the . hills. On the left and right, Roone's possemen emerged from the town in two pursuing columns, their positions restricting the fugitives to only one course.

Don Ricardo dropped back to say brittlely, "They laid a trap for us while we haggled with that pig of a rancher!"

"Good thing you smelled it out." It was a measure of his weariness, Bishop guessed, that he hadn't caught on to it. He hoped his senses weren't dulling. "With more men, Roone could've surrounded the whole town. He's out to capture us alive if he can. It's the hills for us." He looked at Tandra. She was having to ride with one stirrup, her hurt foot hanging free. Troubled by his tone, she met his eyes, and he said strongly, "We'll make it!"

"Their horses are as worn-down as ours," Don Ricardo put in, not to be outdone in offering encouragement.

"Not yours, Rico. The mare can outrun 'em."

The don picked up the lead again without replying. Bishop sent McLean a faint grin, and McLean nodded. A badman, Rico, wily, full of guile and incorrigible vanity and black deviltry. Worth ten good men in a tight pinch. A sticker-to-hell.

The south column of possemen, abreast at a distance, began curving inward. Don Ricardo tried a high, dropping shot, but the range was too far for his gun to place a bullet where he wanted it. Bishop borrowed McLean's rifle, and, concerting his aim to the motion of his horse, cracked off two shots. The column edged respectfully outward, not returning the fire.

"It'll come in useful," Bishop said, handing the rifle back to McLean. "Glad we could buy shells for it."

"Some of them have rifles too."

"They won't use 'em unless it looks like we're getting away. Roone thinks we're worth a lot more to him alive than dead. That blasted silver!"

"But he'd take us in dead for second choice, eh?"

"No argument there, Mac!"

XVIII

THEY RESTED in a fireless, dry camp, in the foothills of the Saddle Mountains, the three men taking turns on watch, letting Tandra sleep. Bishop stretched his long body on the ground, easing its aches and pains.

"You awake, Rico?" he muttered in the dark. Don Ricardo grunted, and Bishop said, "Horses won't be good for much tomorrow. Mine's got some stuff left. And yours. But the other two are about played out."

"So are theirs," the don remarked drowsily. "They couldn't lift them to a lope, that last run we made."

"Tomorrow they'll bring up fresh ones. They know roughly where we are. How's it, McLean?"

McLean, on watch, answered, "Not a sound."

Don Ricardo yawned, and wiped his eyes. "They're resting, like us."

"Yeah. Resting all round us, waiting for light!" Bishop said. "We've got a few hours. Make the most of 'em."

"*Madre de dios!*" The prayerful oath came seldom from the don; he usually called upon a thousand devils, *mil diablos*. "What a *dolorido* you are! Go to sleep!"

"I've slept some. Now I'm thinking."

"Think to yourself! I want to—"

"D'you know these mountains?"

"No."

"Nor me," Bishop admitted, "but these foothills are no good by daylight. Roone will have his men riding all through them. I propose starting over the mountains before morning."

Don Ricardo sat up, wide awake. "In the dark? These mountains? They're all cliffs and barrancas, I know that much about them! The higher you climb, the worse it gets! We would have to leave our horses behind!"

"Can't. Roone would find 'em. He'd know what we're up to."

"But there's no trail, nothing but cliffs and—"

"How d'you know? We might strike an Apache foot trail."

The don laughed hollowly. "Or a goat path!"

"All right," Bishop said, rising to his feet and wincing at the prospect of abusing them once more. "It won't be easy, but it's something to do. Come here, McLean."

He told McLean briefly of his intention. "I'll take Tandra with me. Want to come along?"

McLean looked at the sleeping girl cuddled under the Mexican saddle blankets. "I guess anything beats skulking around these bare hills," he replied slowly, "waiting to be killed or captured." He brought his look back to Bishop, hard, challenging the big man's possessive attitude toward Tandra. "Count me in!"

Don Ricardo got up, slammed his sombrero on, hissed painedly, and cocked it onto the uninjured side of his head. "*Mira!* They'll track us in the morning. And among them there must be some who know these mountains. While we climb and search our way, they—"

"We'll have a start on 'em. Anywhere we have to climb on foot, so will they."

"Yes, but climbing in the dark, not knowing where we—"

"Don't do it, then! Let's split up. The mare's the best mount. You can mosey off with a good chance to get clear by morning. We can't—two horses worn out and the girl lamed." Bishop stooped over Tandra and picked her up, saddle blankets and all. "Get a move on, McLean! Luck to you, Rico!"

"To hell with you!" snorted the don. He tightened the mare's loosened cinch. "I hope this animal is sure-footed."

Bishop lifted the sleep-drugged girl onto her horse. "Take hold of the saddle horn," he bade her, "and don't fall off." She obeyed, barely conscious of what was happening. He mounted the black and drew her horse up alongside by its reins.

"We'll keep to an easy walk," he said. "Oh, you coming with us, Rico?"

"Your irony, if that is what it is, lacks the grace of wit," said Don Ricardo superiorly. He touched the mare forward. "Follow me! Watch over Tandra. McLean, you drop to the rear."

"Is he taking charge of this party?" McLean murmured to Bishop. "He's got his gall!"

"Somebody's got to scout ahead. He's in the best shape to do it."

"What will he do if we get clean out of this? Not much hope of it, I know, but suppose we do?"

Bishop tugged the reins of Tandra's jaded horse, urging it to keep pace with the black. "Well, he's lost all his horses, and he can't believe in the silver. Naturally he wouldn't want to go home empty-handed."

"Naturally?"

"To him it's natural."

"And to you!" McLean grated. "My God, to you and him she's still a—a prize in a contest between you two! Even now!"

Bishop reached out a steadying hand to Tandra, swaying sleepily in her saddle. "Rico understands that," he said.

"It's unhuman!"

"No, it's simple. I'll beat him, or he'll beat me. In the meantime we're working together to, h'm, save the prize. Hang on to your saddle horn, Tandra, hear me?"

McLean, savagely caustic, jealous of Bishop's monopoly of Tandra and her automatic compliance, said, "Sure, take good care of the prize! She's all that's left!"

"You forget the silver."

"Damn the silver! If it wasn't for that, she'd be—"

"She'd be where? Hiding in a cave. It was time she got out of that kind of life. Quit your sorrowing over her."

"The cave was safer!"

"Safe like a jail. Now she's out, three men taking care of her. Many a lonely young lady would settle for that. You don't know women, Mac."

"Maybe not," said McLean. "But I do have human feeling for her! Personal feeling! You and Risa don't!"

"Oh?" Bishop swung his head and stared at him. "You'd be surprised." A scowl creased his black-stubbled jaw. "That goddam remark helps me make up my mind. If we get through this, and I beat Rico out of taking Tandra—I'll keep her!" he stated bluntly. "Now drop to the rear like Rico told you!"

He rode on in a bad humor, trailing after Don Ricardo up the mountain slopes, hearing McLean follow a few lengths behind.

In the heights, yawning ravines abounded, flanked by towering cliffs, as though some mighty cataclysm had shattered the mountains. Ledges and shelves falsely promised passage and led nowhere, petering out at dizzying drops.

Don Ricardo, leading, repeatedly guessed wrong, and they had to back up and retrace their course. He claimed to have an infallible sense of direction; in the giant maze, direction meant nothing. He also claimed that he could see in the dark like a cat; and twice, before the moon came up, he would have ridden over the abrupt edge of a ravine if the mare had let him.

They rode at a walk in single file, surrounded by a dead world of gray walls and gloomy chasms that gave back a score of echoes to each hoofbeat. The mare became balky, swinging its head and fighting the bit, taking dainty little steps sideways from where the don wanted it to go.

"Give the mare her head," Bishop growled, his voice echoing back like a harsh chorus. "She can't do worse than you! We haven't made half a mile in two hours."

Exasperated, Don Ricardo let the mare choose its own course. "Why the devil did anyone name these the Saddle Mountains?" he inquired. The mare turned onto an unpromising ledge, hair-raisingly narrow and winding up, and stepped contentedly along it. "They're a horseman's dream of hell!"

"I'm not even sure now we're in the Saddle Mountains," Bishop said. He sent a look to the rear.

Tandra, wide awake, was closely following him. With the face of the cliff on one side, and a sheer drop on the other, the ledge was guaranteed to keep anybody wakeful. She was not an experienced rider, and Bishop told her to stop fiddling with the reins. Behind her, McLean walked on foot, leading his horse, having learned that it inclined to hug the cliff and bang his knee. He carried his rifle on his shoulder by its sling.

The ledge, winding in and out with the contours of the high cliff, shrank narrower. The horses had to sidle around sharp bends, snuffling nervously. A loose stone, kicked off, could be heard bounding down for long seconds before it hit bottom. The roan mare paced onward, unperturbed and confident; it had either traveled this unlikely route before, or it was following a strong instinct.

"She seems to know the way, Rico."

"If she's fooling us I'll shoot her! We could never back out of here. *Mira!*—there's hardly space to dismount." Don Ricardo reached inside his once-white shirt. "I bought a bottle in that barroom. Tequila." He uncorked it and drank.

"How 'bout passing it back here?"

"Don't crowd up on me! Not here!"

"Thought you had a good head for heights."

"I have. It is my stomach that flutters."

The ledge widened, allowing them better progress, and Don Ricardo then passed the bottle over. Ascending a last grade, they topped out onto an uneven mesa. The don patted the mare's neck. "*Gracias, querida mia!*"

"We'd have made better time if you hadn't argued with her," Bishop said. His humor stayed dour despite the tequila. "Where now?" He saw McLean stop beside Tandra and speak to her in a low tone. "Anything you've got to say, McLean, say it out loud!"

"You're awful proddy," McLean observed. "Look, I didn't want to mention this while we were on the ledge. I don't think I heard anything behind us. If I did—well, I wasn't conscious of it. But I had the feeling we were being trailed."

Bishop and Don Ricardo eyed him. Seasoned campaigners, they paid serious regard to intuitive nudges. "Your hunch could be right," Bishop granted. "Maybe they nosed out our camp when the moon came up. They didn't have to wait for morning. Roone works best at night, I've been told."

Don Ricardo raised a hand. "Listen!"

They fell silent, straining their ears to catch any sound in the vast stillness. Nothing that moved could avoid sending out ripples of reverberating echoes. In a moment the clear night air brought it, a wavering rumor of distant riders.

"You hear it, Rogue?"

"Yeah. They're riding pretty free. Not on the ledge,

any ledge. They probably know a better route than we took. Short cuts." Bishop breathed deeply. "Let the mare have her way, anywhere she goes. She's our guide."

Don Ricardo gently shook his reins. The roan mare trotted across the mesa and unerringly found a downward path that on sight appeared impossible to descend. The horses dropped down after her.

"You called it right, Mac," Bishop said to McLean. "Wish I'd been wrong."

"So do I."

They rode along the stony floor of a deep ravine, filling it with the noise of their clacking hoofbeats. Moonlight washed the west rim like dulled silver, accentuating the darkness below, the sky a jagged slit, star-studded.

"We're coming to a dead end," Don Ricardo called over his shoulder.

The echoes repeated after him, *a dead end—dead end* . . . "A bad end!" intruded a different echo.

"Who was that?"

"Me! United States Special Marshal Arno Roone!"

"Pull up!" Bishop snapped. "Quiet! He can't see us, only hears us. He's up on the east rim, I think."

They drew to a standstill. Roone called down, "You're in a blind gully! You're boxed! Give yourselves up!" He waited only a few seconds after his echoes subsided. "Fire, men!"

Guns crashed along the east rim. The possemen overshot in the dark; their bullets ricocheted off the rock of the west wall. "Now, Rico!" Bishop heeled the black. "Gamble on the mare! Mac, hit up those horses!"

Don Ricardo slapped his reins, and the mare ran on as if to plow full into the dead end of the ravine, but it turned smartly off the stony floor, climbing a dim scrap of game-trail that angled back up the west wall. The firing ceased. A disturbed night bird shrieked.

Roone shouted to his men, "Can any o' you see 'em? What're they doing? I can hear 'em!"

So they weren't acquainted with this particular route. The roan mare, Bishop guessed, must once have belonged to somebody who spent much time in these chopped-up mountains, for reasons best known to himself. Prospecting, perhaps, or hunting game. Or hiding from the law. It could find its way around, though not by known trails.

"I can hear 'em!" Roone repeated. The jumbled echoes made it impossible to locate anything by sound. His voice cracked, shrill in an excess of anxiety that the fugitives might yet escape him. "Where are they?"

They were climbing out of the blind ravine. As they ascended higher, their sounds grew less audible. Below the moonlit rim, Don Ricardo said softly, "Fast!" He lashed the mare. For a short moment they loomed scrambling in the margin of moonlight. Three or four rifles cracked hurriedly. Then they were over the rim, hearing Roone cry out like a distraught woman, "No, no! They can't! Get after 'em round the gully!"

The west rim proved to be no wider than a ridge, a deeper ravine beyond stretching for unknown miles. "So-oo!" Bishop grunted. "Steep as a horse's face! See what the mare makes of it, Rico. Hurry! They're coming round."

The mare dropped off the ridge into black moonshadow. "*Ay de mí!*—another ledge," Don Ricardo called up. "Careful! One misstep and you fall half a mile! This animal must be half mountain goat!"

With snorting difficulty the laboring horses found their footing behind the mare. Although not as narrow as the last one, the ledge canted outward and downward at a fearsome slant. Their hoofs slithered on bare rock. Tandra's horse stalled, trembling. "You've got to prod it on," Bishop told the girl. She slapped it gingerly, trying not to look down into the black abyss. "Harder! Nothing to be afraid of," he said, forgiving himself for the lie. "Don't be afraid."

"I won't be, if you say so." She hit her horse a good smite, and it came on.

"Rogue," murmured Don Ricardo, "you have a way with you! Nothing to be afraid of? Nothing but every bone broken—"

"Don't let the horse hear you."

XIX

SEEMINGLY ENDLESS, neither dipping nor rising, the ledge ran like a crease along the face of the cliff. The ravine itself deepened; at sunrise, boulders far below were pebbles and the dry floor was a wrinkle, thread-thin.

McLean, leading his cliff-hugging horse in the rear, called forward, "They're on foot, all but Roone. Left their horses behind. His must be a mountain pony, like the mare."

"Can you reach 'em with your rifle?" Bishop asked him.

"Not yet. Soon, though. They're gaining. My horse and Tandra's slow us down. And if I shoot, so will they. The men up front with Roone are carrying rifles. This is a bad place for a shoot-out!"

"Couldn't be much worse, but it's got to come to it, unless—"

"Unless what?" McLean rested his eyes on Tandra. "Look, Bishop," he said, "take her up behind you. She's light. Your black's still in shape to outdo them, all but Roone."

Bishop eyed him expressionlessly. "What've you got in mind for yourself?"

"I'll stay here and stand Roone off, and the others."

"You'd take on a posse for us?"

"Not for you. For her." McLean shuttled a somber look at Don Ricardo, and brought it back to Bishop. "I'd expect you to do as much for her, or more. Understand?"

"Sure. Hey, Rico, Mac offers to stay behind. What d'you say to it?"

The don shrugged, nodded. "Why not? His horse is finished. He has a rifle. He is the logical one to do it."

"Yeah, but where's his cover? This ledge is as bare—"

"Mike!" Tandra cried. "Mike, no!"

McLean raised his rifle. He placed the muzzle to the head of his horse and squeezed the trigger. The horse collapsed with only a quivering of its legs. "There's my cover," he said, and got down behind it.

"Mike—!"

"Come on." Bishop took the reins from Tandra's hands. "When your horse gives out I'll take you up behind me. Come on!" he repeated harshly, tugging her horse into step. "Push on, Rico!"

McLean's rifle sounded off before they had gone a hundred yards. Roone drew in, gesturing urgently at the men walking behind his horse. The men eased on by him and crouched in rifle-firing positions, and promptly the ravine boomed the echoes of a dozen reports.

"Your friend is an accommodating young man," Don Ricardo remarked to Bishop.

"That's one way to put it."

After a while the don inquired, with an edge of puzzled irritation, "Why did he do it?" The gunfire was rumbling then like distant thunder. "He owed us nothing. He is not one of us. Was it pride? Was it despair? *Mira!*—I forgot. Tandra, of course! He is romantic. He did it because of—"

"Shut up!" Bishop barked at him.

"*Qué?*"

"Shut up, I said!"

"*Bien, bien!* Our tempers are very bad! I wonder why."

They came upon an offshoot of the ledge, bending upward. The mare unhesitatingly turned onto the upper fork. Minutes later it passed through a notch in the rim and paced sedately out into the open.

South and west the mountains diminished to rolling hills, sunny under the broad blue sky. In the far-off flatlands Bishop picked out a faint ribbon that he thought, from its undeviating straightness, was probably the Hassayampa-Harrisburg stageroad. Don Ricardo gazed gladly about with the air of a man fresh out of prison, until Bishop voiced a question:

"Which of us goes back for McLean?"

The don lowered his eyelids. "Oh, yes, him. Yes, you must take care of your friend. I will wait here with Tandra while you—"

"Cut the cards?"

"Not with you, Rogue!"

"Toss for it?"

"My coin?"

"Nothing doing!"

They regarded each other faithlessly. "One of us must stay with Tandra," Don Ricardo said.

Bishop shook his head. "Her horse could carry her to that stageroad at a walk. A stage will come along sometime. We'll both go back."

"Leave her alone? To go help McLean? That is all wrong! I fancy they have killed him by now, anyway. What can we do for a dead man?"

"We can take up his job and hold 'em off."

"But—"

"Go back for him!" Tandra suddenly burst out, and the two of them blinked at her. "Stop your talk, and hurry!" Her eyes blazed at Don Ricardo. "Are you afraid? Mike wasn't!"

The don flushed darkly. He reined the mare back toward the notch in the rim, saying muffledly, "We both go, damn it!" On the way down the fork, he exclaimed, "Women are the very devil!" And, later, in a warmer tone, "She has spirit! A brave little spitfire, yet as gentle as—"

"Put your tomcat mind on our business," Bishop cut in on his kindling reveries. "I haven't heard a shot in some time."

"No; McLean is dead. We'll ride smack into the posse any minute now. What are we doing? Testing each other's nerve? A childish game! I can turn back without any hurt to my—"

"That would answer the girl's question, all right. 'Are you afraid?' 'No, but I backed out before we got to McLean!'"

"There he is! And the posse! Are you satisfied?"

"Not yet."

McLean lay motionless, the hide of his dead horse ripped and flayed by bullets. Roone and half a dozen of his possemen were edging slowly forward, rifles ready. They evidently were unsure of whether McLean was dead or not, and he must have instilled in them a vigilant respect for his rifle; all their attention was tensely concentrated upon catching a glimpse of him behind the dead horse. McLean's head shifted.

"They've got him pinned down," Bishop said. He leaned forward and hit the mare a terrific whack with the flat of his hand. "Let's get him out, Rico!"

The mare's jump snapped Don Ricardo's head back. He choked on an angry oath, but instantly picked up his involuntary role of a charging rescuer, flipping out a gun and firing. Bishop rode behind him on the ledge, spending shells, like the don, for the sake of creating distraction. Sixguns at that range were speculative; the profit was the shock to taut nerves. Roone and his half-dozen sharpshooters broke off their cautious advance, astonished, instinctively ducking.

McLean twisted his head to stare at Don Ricardo leaping off the mare and darting to him. Roone shouted something that sounded like, "Get 'em!"—his voice tight and thin, a tin trumpet.

Don Ricardo tore the rifle from McLean's hands. He stood up straight, took quick aim, fired. Roone raised his face skyward as if praying. The don emptied the rifle, rapid-fire. A posseman bumped into Roone's horse. Another let his rifle slip, stopped in the act of sighting a shot, and a third lowered himself very carefully to the ground.

Roone gave a violent jerk of his body. Thin lips pressed hard, his face dead white, he flailed an arm to the men in the rear, beckoning them up forward. The motion caused his horse to shy, nearly unseating him. To save his swaying balance he reached for the saddle horn, fumblingly missed grasping it, and bowed over onto the neck of the horse, his boots digging its sides.

The horse went into a broken gallop, an unhandy gait, Roone jolting in the saddle, hanging on, trying to force himself to sit upright and control it. One of the men sprang at its bridle. The horse threw up its head in fright, ramming Roone in the face and breaking his hold. Roone fell off. He struck the lip of the ledge and rolled over it. His scream in mid-air wailed up from the ravine. The men stared aghast at the spot. One, the young man who sprang at the bridle, turned away and threw up.

"Get set to catch the horse, Mac!" Bishop said. "Snap out of it!"

Roone's runaway horse reared, unable to cram through or dodge around them. Don Ricardo, bounding onto the mare, took off as fast as he had come. McLean caught a flying rein of the runaway, and at once Bishop put his black to pounding after the don.

XX

THEY RODE UP through the notch, the black hard behind the mare, and Tandra, waiting, looked stricken by unbearable woe.

"Mike—?"

"He's coming," Bishop said. He saw the glad relief wash the despair from her face, transforming it, and he turned his eyes to Don Ricardo. "Good work, Rico."

The don paid him a frigid glance. "I was driven to it!" He looked frowningly at Tandra; she was listening intently at the notch, her hands tightly clasped. "Is he worth it?" he muttered. "What is he?"

"A treasure hunter."

"What?"

"Rambles around hunting for valuables that have been hidden away, buried, lost or whatever. It's a chronic habit with some people, like prospecting for gold. The big strike's always just over the next hill."

Don Ricardo fingered his chin musingly. "Does he ever find any treasure?"

McLean, riding Roone's horse, came up out of the notch. Tandra leaned from her saddle toward him, arms unashamedly open. He drew alongside and they wordlessly embraced.

"On this trip," Bishop answered the don, "he's come close to it."

"You make a joke?"

"I never felt less like making a joke in my life."

"*Ay, ay! Qué dolor!*" The don's dark eyes glimmered a hard mockery. "Treasure is for those who can take and hold it, no?"

"It generally works out that way."

The pair drew apart, and Bishop said to them, "Make

your way down to that stageroad yonder. Take your time and spare the horses, or you'll be afoot."

"There's a mighty sore posse coming along the ledge," McLean told him.

"We'll take care of that."

Don Ricardo watched the pair ride off at a walk. He held his smooth, slightly blunted features in repose, while the glimmer in his eyes brightened. "And what, may I ask," he inquired with silky overpoliteness, "is the reason for that generous action?"

"He covered our getaway. We do the same for him."

"I consider the debt paid."

"Don't be so damned cheap!" Bishop dismounted. So did the don. "I haven't any particular objection to covering his getaway. Letting him take the girl, however, is quite another matter. Permit me to point out," he continued elaborately, "that she is not your property, to give as you wish."

"Nor yours."

"Treasure is for— But I have said that before. *Bien,* he will not get far with her. You have considered that, no doubt. The gift is not meant to be permanent, eh?"

"That remains to be seen."

They reloaded their guns, scrupulously keeping the muzzles pointed earthward, and stepped to the mouth of the notch, one on each side of it.

"We're not trying to wipe out a posse—" Bishop began.

"And we do not plan on an all-day siege," said Don Ricardo, glancing after McLean and Tandra. "So?"

"Let's both shoot fast soon's we hear 'em."

"Show them what we can do, yes. I can get twelve shots off in five seconds. You?"

"I've done it in four. Not with these guns, though; they're a shade stiff."

Waiting, they listened to a murmur of sound that resolved into clumping footfalls on the ledge below. The noise of the tramping men changed, growing more distinct; they were coming up the fork. The don cocked an eyebrow at Bishop, who nodded.

Their four guns roared together, shot following shot as rapidly as the hammers could be cocked and triggers squeezed. The ravine boomed, magnifying the deafening racket, multiplying the discharges and the droning whirrs of bullets ricocheting off rock.

After the last shots, the echoes rumbled back and forth off down the ravine, leaving a stunned silence.

"Goddam!" said a retreating voice. "Anybody wants that, they're welcome! I'm a married man, an'— Hey, don't crowd me off this ledge!"

Bishop listened to the men jostling one another down the fork. They were going back, shaken by the murderous blast of concentrated gunfire. They didn't have Roone to nag and harry them on with his greed for bounty, his lust for revenge, his hatred.

"Rico," he said, "I held out on you." He holstered an empty gun, kept the other in his hand, cocked, finger on the trigger. "I left one shell unfired."

Don Ricardo smiled wickedly at him. "So did I!"

The don held his gun pointed upward, arm bent; a duelist's stance. "Were you going to shoot me, Rogue?"

"Only if you went after those two," Bishop replied. "I still don't advise it. You've got a clear route to Mexico. Take it!"

"Why?"

"You killed a U.S. marshal. The posse saw it."

The don shrugged lightly, his eyes fixed on Bishop's. "I am not going into mourning for him! Give me another reason."

"It makes you a marked man, more than ever. Tomorrow they'll all be out looking for you. Federal men. Army men. And the bounty hunters."

"I have been hunted half my life. You are surely not concerned for my safety!" The don dipped a swift look at Bishop's gun. "We have one shell each. Do we kill each other over a woman?"

"It's up to you," Bishop said, and sent an opaque stare in the direction of McLean and Tandra. "We don't move from here till we've got it settled." The stageroad was a long way off, an empty trace through an empty land.

"I have a strange feeling that there is something more involved. Something I have overlooked in all the haste and rush and confusion."

"Something you've discounted, you mean."

"Do I?" Don Ricardo contemplated Bishop uncertainly. He took a different tack, asking, How did you happen to couple up with McLean?"

"By chance, more or less. We had a run-in. He was on the track of a big find. I got him out of a tough spot, and cut myself in for a share."

"What are you saying? That there actually is a load of *contrabando* silver hidden in that ghost town?"

"Piles of it. In those rawhide sacks they used to pack it in. Some have split open from the weight of it. That's how I got those pesos I shoved in your face."

Don Ricardo absently touched his bruised face. "It sounds more believable now. McLean, a treasure hunter. You—I know your way of cutting yourself in on anything profitable! *Madre de dios!*" he breathed. "And McLean knows the hiding place?"

Bishop shook his head. "No. I do. You heard me tell Roone where it is, didn't you?"

"Yes, yes, but who knows when to believe you? A good thing I shot Roone! That leaves only you and me knowing the cache. You had two reasons for holding out a shell on me, Rogue! Tandra and the silver!" The don's forefinger stroked the trigger of his upraised gun. "I understand you better each time we meet! Winner take all, eh? All or nothing, let the loser go hang!"

"I don't play for fun. Neither do you."

"True! I should have known you were onto a gainful

155

something in the ghost town. What threw me off was your offer to me—a fortune in silver pesos, no less! I could not treat it seriously, under those circumstances. And yet—"

"Want to spend your shell?" Bishop asked, tilting his gun an inch upward. "Then we'll both lose all!"

"No," replied the don, matching Bishop's move by bringing his gun slightly downward. "No, but I now accept your offer of the silver. Your share of it."

"I offered it for the girl," Bishop reminded him. "It was a deal."

"That," Don Ricardo sighed pensively, "is so. We will abide by it. This is one time we split the winnings between us, friend Rogue!"

"How'll we work it?"

"We put up our guns, and part here, in mutual good faith and, er, trust. You have purchased Tandra, practically speaking. What you do about McLean is your affair. He and she show all the signs of being—"

"How about you?" Bishop broke in curtly.

"I shall go to Mexico, gather some reliable men, make a fast trip to Bronco City, and collect the silver."

"My half of it, you mean. Leave the rest of it there."

"Oh, of course, of course! Only your half, Rogue. Be assured of that! For me to take it all would be, er—"

"Hoggish," Bishop supplied.

"*Qué?*"

"Like a pig."

The don inclined his head in agreement. "Like a winner taking all! H'm, your gun—"

"I'm easing the hammer down. You do the same."

They holstered their guns. "Would you have gone through with it?" the don asked curiously. "Shot it out with me?"

"Don't you doubt it!"

"H'm!" Don Ricardo swung lithely aboard the roan

mare. "I think some say we will. Until then—*adios, Roguel*"

Bishop nodded. He watched him ride at a canter down the descending hills, away from the tracks of McLean and Tandra, his richly embroidered sombrero aslant on the uninjured side of his head. A special kind of man, Rico. Dangerous enemy, most reliable side-kick in desperate times. Wily as a lobo, tricky as a fox. Reckless as a death-singing Comanche.

Well, the day would come. Some bitter day of final conflict, two gunfighters dying in a hushed street, or the desert, the mountains. Knowing at last, too late, they were brothers; two of a kind, kindred. Too well matched, each, to tolerate the other.

He would regret it. They both would regret it.

He rode after McLean and Tandra. Catching up with them, he said, "My feet won't be right for a month."

McLean gave him a guarded look. "Where's Risa going?"

"Mexico."

"He's quit?"

"You don't know Rico! No, he's going there to get another gang. Then he'll run up to Bronco City for the silver, where I told him to look, down behind the Morning Glory."

"Is that where it is?" McLean asked, surprised at nothing that Bishop might have discovered.

"That's where he thinks it is. Give him a week or so to scrabble in that broken glass," Bishop said, "and *then* he'll quit and go home. It's not there."

"Then you don't know where Grandy's silver is hidden?" Tandra asked him, and McLean shrugged, saying it didn't matter; money was only money. A million Mexican pesos, give or take a hundred thousand or two...

"I didn't say that. Yes, I know." Bishop paused. Between Tandra's plaintive question and McLean's disrespectful attitude toward hard cash, there existed a

157

wide gap. Women, he had noted, generally showed the best sense of material values.

"I understand some Navajo," he said. "Your uncle didn't, Mac. When Navajo Jones proposed that they cache the silver under Clear Day, he was giving the Navajo name for Bronco Rock. It didn't occur to me when I read the letter, but what he must've said was 'Kleea Doy,' which in Navajo means Bad Horse. Kleea Doy, Bad Horse—Bronco Rock. Your uncle thought he said Clear Day. Maybe he had a tin ear. They cached the silver right under Bronco Rock, in a safe place Navajo Jones knew of. I guess they used ropes, or rigged up ladders."

"Did you work that out in your head?" McLean asked somewhat skeptically.

"Not till I dived into that crevice, after your bullet cut the rope," Bishop admitted. "I fell all over the silver in there."

"You didn't tell me then."

"I'm telling you now. It's there!"

McLean and Tandra were staring at him, slowly grasping what his words meant. He said, "If you want to stay legal, go see the territorial governor about it. You don't need to give any details, only that you've found a cache of Mexican silver. It won't be confiscated, but it'll be impounded till things like federal duties are squared. Maybe you'll only come out with half of it, clear. That's still plenty. Do I see a stage coming?" He peered off at a feather of dust moving up from the south. "The Harrisburg mail express, probably. You catch it."

McLean swallowed, and found his voice. "I made a deal with you! Half the silver's yours!"

"That," Bishop growled, "is too high a price for a drink of water. From what you come out clear with, bank a tenth part for me in the Wells Fargo at Tucson. I'll round in one day and pick it up, after things have cooled off." From his money belt he dug out a wad of

158

banknotes. "You'll need some cash to go on till you get straightened out. It's a loan."

In a small voice, Tandra asked him, "You don't want me to—to stay with you?"

"No," he said. "Get on down to the road and catch that stage. Have a doctor see to her foot, Mac, and your shoulder. Buy new clothes. Make yourselves presentable for the governor."

He looked after them, riding slowly together to the stageroad. "Sure," he muttered. "You could've stayed. I could've hogged the silver. We'd have had a hell of a high time."

He shrugged, dismissing the picture. It had flaws in it. *You gotta live up to y'self . . .* Well, he had come out ahead of Rico, anyway.

Winners of the SPUR and WESTERN HERITAGE AWARD

Awarded annually by the Western Writers of America, the Golden Spur is the most prestigious prize a Western novel, or author, can attain.

☐	29743-9	GOLD IN CALIFORNIA Tod Hunter Ballard	$1.95
☐	30267-X	THE GREAT HORSE RACE Fred Grove	$2.25
☐	47083-1	THE LAST DAYS OF WOLF GARNETT Clifton Adams	$2.25
☐	47493-4	LAWMAN Lee Leighton	$2.25
☐	55124-6	MY BROTHER JOHN Herbert Purdum	$2.25
☐	82137-5	THE TRAIL TO OGALLALA Benjamin Capps	$2.25
☐	85904-6	THE VALDEZ HORSES Lee Hoffman	$2.25

Available wherever paperbacks are sold or use this coupon.

◖ ACE CHARTER BOOKS
P.O. Box 400, Kirkwood, N.Y. 13795

Please send me the titles checked above. I enclose $ _____.
Include $1.00 per copy for postage and handling. Send check or money order only. New York State residents please add sales tax.

NAME_____

ADDRESS_____

CITY_____STATE_____ZIP_____

A–2

NAME _____

ADDRESS _____

CITY _____ STATE _____ ZIP _____

A-2